THE *Heart* OF
THE *Matter*

STORIES *from* HOPE HAVEN

THE *Heart* OF THE *Matter*

LESLIE GOULD

Guideposts
New York, New York

www.guideposts.com
(800) 932-2145
Guideposts Books & Inspirational Media

Cover design and illustration by Lookout Design, Inc.
Interior design by Lorie Pagnozzi
Typeset by Aptara

Printed and bound in the United States of America
10 9 8 7 6 5 4 3 2 1

To Peter—
husband, father, nurse, and soldier.

Acknowledgments

Many thanks to my husband Peter for his expertise in the medical field. Any misses are mine—and all hits are his. Thank you, too, to Peter and to Libby Salter for reading the manuscript in its first draft. I couldn't have done it without both of you.

A big acknowledgment to all the nurses in my life. I treasure your stories and your service to others.

Thank you to my agent Chip MacGregor for his dedication, to my editor Lindsay Guzzardo for her insight and to the entire Guideposts team for their vision and attention to detail.

"Man looks at the outward appearance, but the Lord looks at the heart."

—1 Samuel 16:7 (NIV)

THE *Heart* OF THE *Matter*

Chapter One

BATTERED TULIPS, BEATEN DOWN BY THE RAIN, bowed alongside the road as Anabelle Scott slowed for the city limits of Deerford. A tiny streak of pink appeared on the eastern horizon, signaling the dawn, and by the looks of the steel gray sky, it might be the most dramatic evidence of the sun all day.

By the time she turned onto Jeffries Street and pulled behind Hope Haven Hospital—something she had been doing for the last thirty years—the rain was blowing sideways, pelting her car and swaying the budding trees toward the ground. Even though March had ended and April begun, the coming of spring still roared like a lion through northern Illinois.

She parked in the staff lot, pushed open the car door, and held her hood over her head as she forced the door shut with her foot. Before she could start her rush toward the entrance, a movement in the far corner of the parking lot caught her attention. There was Eddie Blaine wearing insulated coveralls and standing on a ladder, scrubbing the concrete wall. Was that graffiti?

She hurried toward him, dodging the puddles and streams of water crisscrossing the lot. "Eddie," she called. "It's too stormy for you to be out here!"

He held a wire brush midair and turned toward her, his broad shoulders squared. Black paint had been sprayed in broad strokes across the wall. "I think I'm going to have to power wash it."

"In this weather?"

Eddie lifted the brush in a gesture of defeat. "It sends a bad message to leave it. They say graffiti begets more graffiti. At least that's what the policeman who took the report said a little while ago."

Who'd ever target the hospital? This is terrible.

She was about to voice her thoughts when a gust of wind nearly knocked her off balance. "Eddie—," she was going to tell him he needed to get indoors, that it was crazy to be out in the middle of a storm, but she knew it wouldn't make any difference. The man was as dedicated to the care of the hospital as the nurses and doctors were dedicated to their patients. "Take care," she called out instead.

He pulled his stocking cap down over his ears, still holding the brush in his hand, and then waved as he smiled.

Anabelle increased her stride toward the hospital, buttoning the top of her coat with her free hand and then pulling her hood back in place, as James Bell steered his minivan into the lot. As usual, he looked upbeat but also tired. That might not be so unusual at six thirty in the morning, but she couldn't help wondering how he was doing under the stress of caring for Fern and all that was involved in raising two teenaged boys.

Anabelle was grateful to be entering a new stage of life: in five weeks or so, she would be a grandmother.

As she reached the sidewalk, James caught up with her, the hood of his raincoat pulled over his graying hair, and said a quick hello as he reached to open the door. He froze a moment, his gaze beyond her. "Is that Ainslee's car?"

Anabelle turned. A red Honda Civic was parked in the ER lot. She squinted through the rain. The antenna had a Mickey Mouse on the top, compliments of Ainslee's husband Doug. "Oh dear," Anabelle said, rushing through the door.

"She's probably fine," James said as he followed.

Anabelle pushed her hood from her head and turned toward the ER. Doug could be the one who was ill, not Ainslee. *Oh, Lord,* she silently prayed, *don't let it be either one,* but her heart told her it was her daughter—and the baby. She pushed through the side door to the ER with James behind her and rushed past the reception desk.

"Ainslee!" she called out. "Where are you?"

A plaid curtain halfway down the hall began to flutter and a moment later Doug peered around it. He had a baseball cap pulled tight on his head and an old sweatshirt and jeans on. He looked exhausted.

"What's wrong?" Anabelle practically flew down the hall.

"We don't know yet." Doug began batting at the curtain, and as he did Anabelle grabbed hold of it and yanked it to the side.

Ainslee sat in the middle of the bed. Her legs were crossed, and her dark red hair was twisted in a knot on top of her head. "Hello, Mother." Her eyes were dull and tired.

"What's the matter, honey?"

"I was having some pains, that's all." Ainslee wore a long-sleeved shirt of Doug's over her third-trimester bump.

James's deep voice came from behind her as he said hello and shook Doug's hand.

"What did the doctor say?" Anabelle stepped closer to the bed.

"We just got here," Doug answered.

Anabelle took her daughter's hand. "Are you cramping?"

Ainslee shook her head. "No."

"What's your blood pressure?"

"No one's taken it yet," Doug answered.

Anabelle eyed the blood pressure cuff hanging on a pole. There were so many possibilities—early labor, toxemia, a distressed fetus. "Where does it hurt, exactly?"

Ainslee touched her diaphragm with her free hand, resting it on top of her belly. "Up here. I couldn't sleep all night. I've never felt so miserable."

"Are you sure it's not heartburn?"

"I haven't eaten anything that would cause it."

"Sweetie, why didn't you call me?" Anabelle squeezed her daughter's hand.

Ainslee looked past her mother to Doug. "We didn't want to worry you if it turned out to be nothing."

"Worry me? What are you talking about? That's what mothers are for."

James cleared his throat. "I'm going to go," he said to Anabelle. "I'll stop by CCU and tell them you'll be late." He said his good-byes, and Anabelle thanked him for—she wasn't sure what. Maybe just for caring.

"You should call Dr. Carpenter. In fact—" Anabelle stepped toward the phone in the corner. "I can call her right now."

"It's okay," Ainslee said. "Doug was just about to do it. You should go on up to work."

Anabelle stopped, her hand posed to pick up the phone. "It's fine. Everyone will understand."

Ainslee scooted farther back on the bed, sitting up straighter. "I'm fine—feeling better already."

"You're *not* fine. You're in the ER."

Anabelle looked to Doug for help, but he glanced at Ainslee, then at the floor, and then back at Anabelle and grimaced.

"All right," Anabelle said, dropping her hand to her side. Ainslee had always been the independent sort, not wanting to cause unnecessary fuss, so it was no surprise that she wanted to navigate this alone. But still it was hard for Anabelle to let her.

"I'll stop by and let you know what the doctor says," Ainslee said through a yawn, "before I leave."

Anabelle leaned forward, kissed her daughter on the forehead, and then patted her belly, the cotton shirt soft on her hand, her daughter's abdomen taut. She felt a flutter of joy in her heart before being hit with the ever-present anxiety of worrying about her children—and soon-to-be grandchild.

She pulled her hand away. "Make sure and let me know—call upstairs if you need to. I can come down in a flash." She ducked between the curtains and hurried down the hall, glancing at her watch. She had eight minutes to get changed and be ready to take report. She increased her pace, pushing through the fire door toward the back stairs.

"Here I am," Anabelle said, a little out of breath as she slipped through the cardiac staff door. Debbie, the night charge nurse, sat at the head of the table.

"How's Ainslee?" Debbie's voice was soft. "James told us."

"I don't know," Anabelle said, lowering herself to a chair, her coffee cup in her hand.

"Is it the baby?" Barbara, the unit secretary, asked.

Anabelle's throat constricted. "Maybe."

There was a moment of silence and then Debbie continued with report. Anabelle willed herself to listen to concentrate on the words of her colleagues and to stop obsessing about Ainslee and the baby.

At 11:45 AM, Anabelle tried to call her husband again. She'd already left two messages, but she had no hope that Cameron would check their voice mail. He most likely was out in the barn puttering around. She didn't bother to leave a third message. After she hung up the phone, she tried to fathom why it would take Ainslee more than five hours in the ER as she turned her attention to the staff schedule.

Anabelle stared at the computer screen for a long moment. She had never been tempted before to check the records of a patient who wasn't hers; it was strictly against policy, even though it was her daughter. She could lose her job if she gave in. She stood to distract herself and decided to grab a cup of coffee, telling Barbara that she would be right back. A quick trip to the staff lounge would loosen her up a little.

As she raced up the steps, the draft coming from the stairwell chilled her. She was still shivering as she pushed through the door of the lounge and nearly collided with her friend Elena.

"Anabelle." Elena's blinding white smile lit up her face for a moment, but then it grew serious. "Are you all right?"

Anabelle wrinkled her nose, not sure if she should talk about her worries.

"What is it?" Elena stepped back, welcoming Anabelle into the vacant lounge.

Anabelle inhaled and then, as she filled her coffee cup and tore open the packet of sweetener, told Elena that Ainslee was in the ER. "But that's all I know," Anabelle said. "She didn't want me to stay down there with her."

Elena's dark brown eyes were kind. "I'm sure she'll be up soon to tell you what's going on. She knows you're worried about your grandchild." Elena had been a grandmother for the last five years, although she was quite a few years younger than Anabelle. "In the meantime, give her space."

Anabelle cringed. Her children had deemed her a "hoverer," but she really was trying to do her best.

Elena added, "And she's probably sleep deprived."

That was probably true. Anabelle took a sip of coffee. Both Doug and Ainslee looked like they hadn't slept at all.

"Not to change the subject, but I'm glad I bumped into you." Elena pulled her sweater tighter. "I've been bouncing ideas around—grandbaby shower ideas." Elena grinned.

"A what?" Anabelle tilted her head.

Elena chuckled. "A grandbaby shower! For your first grand-baby. In fact, I want to honor both you and Ainslee. A joint grandbaby–baby shower."

"I've never heard of such a thing." Anabelle marveled how Elena could always find a reason to throw a party.

"I know. It's original." Elena took a little bow. "Guests could bring things for you to have for the baby at your house—toys, sippy cups, things like that. And lotions and bath salts for Ainslee. Does that make sense?"

"I see," Anabelle said brightening at the idea. It actually sounded like a lot of fun. "Thank you."

"I'll invite women you both know from the hospital and the quilting guild."

"How nice." Anabelle paused. "But you know, we should wait—"

"Of course. Let me know how she is, but don't worry. Chances are everything is fine," Elena said. Anabelle wondered how she could *not* worry about her daughter.

Elena glanced at her watch. "I need to get back to ICU. We have a patient coming up from ER. Things have been crazy down there, really." She hurried out the door.

Anabelle topped off her coffee and headed down the stairs, hoping that Ainslee would be waiting for her at the nurses' station. She wasn't and Barbara said that she hadn't been by. Anabelle slumped down into her chair, stared at the computer screen again, and then turned her attention to the swing-shift assignments.

An hour later, she glanced at the clock for the hundredth time that morning and then toward the doorway. If she didn't hear from one of them in five minutes, she would call Doug's cell phone. If he didn't answer she would march on down and find out for herself.

As she logged off the computer, Barbara whispered, "Look who's here."

Anabelle's head shot up. Ainslee walked toward her, her down jacket in her hands in front of her belly. Anabelle tried to read her daughter's face.

"How are you?"

"It's all right. I'm fine. The baby's fine." She tried to stifle a yawn.

"Where's Doug?"

"He decided to go into the office for a few hours."

That sounded good. Things couldn't be too serious if he'd gone into work, even for a while. "What's going on? What did the doctor say?" Anabelle asked.

Ainslee glanced at Barbara and then whispered, "I'll tell you later."

"I want to hear everything. Do you have time for lunch?"

Ainslee tilted her head and a strand of hair came loose from her haphazard bun and brushed against her face. She tucked it behind her ear. "I am hungry."

"There's a good pasta bar on Mondays."

Ainslee turned toward the clock on the wall and then back. "Boy, I was down there a long time. No wonder I'm starving." It was a quarter past twelve. "Can we go right now?"

"Sure." Anabelle logged off the computer and turned to Barbara. "I'll be about a half hour," she said. "Page me if you need me."

The secretary gave Anabelle one of her all-knowing smiles. "See you when you get back."

Anabelle and Ainslee headed to the cafeteria, where Anabelle filled her plate with salad while Ainslee cruised the pasta bar. Anabelle was doing her best not to beg her daughter to tell her what was going on. She repeated Elena's words—*give her space*—silently as she reached the checkout register and then asked the cashier to ring Ainslee's food up with hers. Anabelle smiled at the sight of her daughter's tray, which was heaped with pasta, a salad, bread sticks, custard, and a carton of milk. There was once a time that she could eat like that too, but it was long, long ago. As she tucked her wallet back into her purse, Anabelle spotted a cup of coffee on Ainslee's tray.

"I bet you can't wait to get back to drinking regular."

Ainslee lifted her tray. "This is regular."

"Sweetie." Anabelle accidentally jostled her purse against her tray and then steadied it. "The caffeine isn't good for the baby."

"No, I think it's fine."

"Honey, I know it's not." Anabelle led the way to the far booth before Ainslee could answer. When Anabelle was pregnant, she hadn't been allowed a drop of regular coffee—only decaf. She settled onto the bench seat, hoping the privacy would encourage a heart-to-heart conversation. Ainslee arrived a moment later.

"I think things have changed since you were pregnant," Ainslee said, sliding onto the opposite bench. "You know," she said with a teasing tone, "it has been a long time."

Anabelle chuckled. In some ways it didn't seem like it had been that long ago—and she'd said her piece, so she'd drop it for now; but she was positive Ainslee shouldn't have caffeine. Why would she want to stimulate the baby?

"Thanks for the food." Ainslee shoved her jacket toward the wall. "I don't think I could have made it home, I'm so hungry."

"They didn't feed you in the ER?" Anabelle pulled a couple of napkins from the dispenser along the wall and handed one to Ainslee.

"They held off in case I needed to have tests."

Elena waved from across the room and hurried toward them. "Is everything okay?" she asked as she approached.

Ainslee shifted on the bench and then looked straight at her mother as she spoke. "Word travels fast around here, doesn't it?" Ainslee put down her fork and smiled at Elena. "I'm fine," she said. "So is the baby." She patted her belly and then took a sip of milk.

Elena waited for a second as if she expected more of an explanation and then said, "Did your mom tell you I want to give you two a baby shower?"

A puzzled expression crossed Ainslee's face. "Doug and me?"

Elena laughed. "No. You and your mom."

"Oh."

Anabelle dabbed at the corner of her mouth with her napkin. Suddenly a joint shower seemed like a horrible idea. Was Ainslee thinking her mother was trying to take advantage of what should be her experience alone?

Elena smiled broadly. "Think about a date—we should do it soon." Elena glanced at Ainslee's belly and smiled. "Within a few weeks or so, right?"

Ainslee nodded.

"The Hope Haven nurses will be thrilled and so will the quilting guild. We all want to celebrate with you and your mom."

"Thank you for being so thoughtful, Elena," Ainslee said and wiggled out of the bench and hugged Elena.

Elena explained that she was going to fill a tray and take it up to the Intensive Care Unit and then said she would be in touch soon.

"That's nice of her," Anabelle said. "Wanting to give a shower." She didn't say "give us" a shower on purpose.

Ainslee wrinkled her nose. "Had you and Elena already talked about this?"

"She just mentioned it this morning." Anabelle placed her napkin in her lap. "Are you okay with the idea? Because—"

"It's fine."

Anabelle took a bite of salad, wondering if she should pry Ainslee more or let it go, but before she decided, Candace came around the corner.

"There you are," she said, her highlighted hair bobbing against her neck. "How are you doing?"

Ainslee blushed and squeaked, "Fine."

Candace turned to Anabelle. "Dr. Carpenter had me go down and check on Ainslee in the ER."

Maybe Ainslee had listened to Anabelle's suggestion to call Dr. Carpenter after all.

"So you're feeling fine?" Candace asked, turning her attention back to Ainslee.

"Good. Starving."

Candace laughed. "Eat. Don't let me stop you."

Ainslee plunged her fork back into the pasta.

"But go easy on the red sauce. That might make the indigestion come back."

"Indigestion?" Anabelle sputtered.

Ainslee's face turned redder.

Candace smiled and tucked a strand of hair behind her ear. "You know I had a couple of bad bouts when I was pregnant with Brooke too. It's amazing how the most common thing can be a really big deal when you're pregnant." Candace seemed oblivious to Ainslee's embarrassment and to Anabelle's shock. "Okay, well, it was good to see you, regardless of the circumstances. I just hope I'm working when you deliver."

Ainslee said she hoped the same, and then Candace said a quick good-bye.

"Indigestion?" Anabelle asked again.

Ainslee's voice was nearly a whisper. "Mother."

"Why didn't you call me?" Anabelle felt embarrassed that her daughter would go to the ER because of indigestion, for just a second, but then it suddenly seemed hilarious and she stifled a laugh.

"Mother." Ainslee shook her head.

"You should have called me, honey. Even if it was the middle of the night." Anabelle was overcome with relief. It was only indigestion. Ainslee and the baby really were fine. "I'm always available."

"Please stop," Ainslee said, her fork in midair. "You know why I didn't call?"

Anabelle shook her head. And she probably didn't want to know.

"Because I feel like you're always criticizing me."

"What do you mean?"

"It's implied in all the advice you're always dishing out."

"I'm just trying to share what I've already learned, as a nurse and a mom." She paused. "Ains, I'm just trying to help."

Ainslee slid back from the table and leaned against the back of the bench, exhaling loudly.

"Eat." Anabelle pointed her fork at her daughter's plate. "You and the baby both need it."

"I'm not hungry anymore." Ainslee slipped into her coat and grabbed her purse. "I need to go get cleaned up and go into work."

"You need a nap, sweetie. That's what you need."

Ainslee stood. "You're doing it again."

Anabelle cringed.

"Mother, I'm twenty-nine years old."

Anabelle pushed her tray to the middle of the table and stood too. "I don't mean to, honestly." Someday Ainslee would understand, someday when her baby was grown. "I'll call you when I get off work, to see how you are." Anabelle reached out to hug her daughter, and Ainslee relaxed for just a moment but then pulled back and picked up her tray with the barely touched food and the untouched coffee, resting it on her belly.

Anabelle sat back down and watched her daughter walk toward the rack of dirty trays. Ainslee slid hers into the slot and then turned and waved. She looked exhausted.

Anabelle took another bite of salad, upset by Ainslee's proclamation. She'd behaved beautifully all morning. She'd stayed out of the ER, and for goodness' sake, it *had* turned out to be heartburn. She'd been right all along. She could have diagnosed it over the phone at 2:00 AM and saved Ainslee a morning at the hospital.

But she couldn't control her kids, not Ainslee or Kirstie or Evan. She'd known that for years. But becoming a grandparent was new territory for her. She felt so protective of this new baby. She smiled in spite of herself. She was going to be a grandmother! She couldn't wait. Ainslee would come around once she had a good night's sleep.

Chapter Two

*D*AD, WE'RE GOING TO BE LATE." NELSON STOOD with his hand on the doorknob of the front door of the Bell home, holding his father's raincoat in his hand and his Boy Scout book in the other. At fourteen, Nelson was slight, like his mother Fern, and his blue eyes were as lively and intense as his dad's.

James bumped against Fern's walker and then bent down and kissed her on the lips. She reclined on the couch, tucked under a cotton blanket with her CD player at her side, listening to an audiobook. "I'll be right back," he said. "The assistant scoutmaster's filling in for me tonight and will give Nelson a ride home."

"Where's Gideon?" Fern turned her head toward James. Her short pixie cut stuck up a little at the crown of her head.

James wasn't sure where their oldest son was, but he didn't want Fern to worry. "He'll be home soon." He probably had stayed after school to study or had a Junior ROTC meeting that James had forgotten about. "If you're awake, ask him to set the table when he gets here."

"Will do." Fern's brown eyes looked heavy, and James hoped that she would doze before dinner. A nap late in the afternoon made the evening easier for her. Wednesday, she had an appointment with Dr. Andrews in Chicago and then an MRI.

Nelson handed James his coat and they hurried out into the rain. It had been pouring all day, but the rain had finally slowed to a drizzle. James started the van, turned the wipers on, and backed out of the driveway. The Boy Scout meeting was across town at their church.

"We're working on our adventure badge," Nelson said.

James nodded. They'd talked about it at the last meeting. He was proud of both of his sons and their community involvement, Nelson in Scouting and Gideon in JROTC. Both programs were teaching them what it meant to be men.

"Hey, there's Gideon," Nelson said, pointing down a side street.

James hesitated, wondering why Gideon would be this far from both the house and his school. He turned the van to the right. Gideon and another boy James didn't recognize were on the sidewalk, headed toward them. James slowed and then stopped the van, opening his window. "Hop in, I'll give you a ride."

Gideon flipped his sweatshirt hood off his head, showing his fresh buzz cut. "No, thank you," he said. He stood straight and tall.

"Who's your friend?" James asked, consciously not commenting on how soaked Gideon's jacket was. He had a perfectly good raincoat. Why didn't he wear it?

"This is Justin Barnes. Justin, this is my dad and my brother Nelson." Gideon seemed uncomfortable as he spoke. "Justin's new at school."

James stuck his hand out the window and Justin stepped forward, the hood of his sweatshirt still up. He shook James's hand, but his grip was weak, not the strong shake James had taught his boys. Justin stepped back quickly.

"We're headed to the house," Gideon said and then moved closer to the van. "Is it okay if Justin stays for dinner?" Gideon spoke quietly, following the family rule from when the boys were young that they couldn't ask permission to invite someone over within hearing distance of the friend.

James inhaled, thinking through the dinner menu. Enchiladas, salad, and chips. Chocolate pudding for dessert. There should be enough. "Sure." He kept his voice low. "But set the table when you get home, and don't wake up Mom if she's asleep. And you'll still be expected to clean up after dinner."

Gideon nodded.

"Good to meet you, Justin," James said, his voice louder. "We'll see you soon."

Justin nodded but didn't speak. James waved at Gideon and then pulled into a driveway to turn around.

"It's already four thirty," Nelson said, pointing at the clock on the dash. "Now I'm really going to be late."

Two hours later, James pulled the enchiladas from the oven as Nelson banged through the front door. "Dad!" he called out.

James placed the pan on top of the stove and stepped through the kitchen doorway. "*Shh.*" He pointed to Fern and then whispered, "How was the meeting?"

Nelson lowered his voice. "Great. I'm almost finished with my badge. I just need to go deep-sea diving or hot-air ballooning."

James grinned. "Can I come along?" There were other things Nelson would have to do for his badge—like go on a hike or canoe on Bass Lake.

Nelson's eyes twinkled as he set his Scout book down on the table that Gideon had already set.

Fern stirred on the couch and her cat Sapphire jumped from where she had been lounging beside her mistress's feet. The cat's raccoonlike tail pointed straight upward as she landed on the floor.

James bent down beside Fern. "Sweetheart," he said, "it's time for dinner."

She opened her eyes and smiled at him. "Give me a minute to wash up."

"Sure," he said. As James put the salad and chips on the table, he watched Fern out of the corner of his eye. Sapphire rubbed against the walker as Fern gripped the handles and pulled herself up. Her first steps were slow, but she picked up speed as she made her way to the hall, her thin frame stooped forward just a little. The cat walked beside her, like a bodyguard.

James called up the stairs to Gideon and Justin that it was time to eat and then asked Nelson to help him put the food on the table.

"What homework do you have?" James asked.

"Language Arts. We're reading *The Outsiders*. Have you heard of it?" Nelson asked.

James chuckled. "I read it way back when."

Nelson seemed surprised. "It's a pretty cool story."

James nodded. Although Deerford didn't have problems with gangs and rivalries as depicted in the novel, he knew any kid could relate to the feeling of not belonging.

A few minutes later, they were all gathered around the table. Justin still had his hood on his head, and James cleared his throat. Gideon knew what his dad was getting at and muttered, "No hats at the table."

"Oh. Sorry," Justin said, flipping his hood off, revealing shoulder-length dark hair that was tucked behind his ears.

As the rest of them folded their hands, Justin reached for the enchiladas.

"Um, we pray first." Gideon's words were barely decipherable.

Justin apologized again, looked around the table and then folded his hands quickly, a wave of red spreading from his neck to his forehead.

"No worries," James said. "I'll say the blessing." He thanked the Lord for food and friendship, and asked for health and good appointments for Fern the day after next. He kept the prayer short and as soon as he finished, nudged the enchiladas closer to Justin. The boy muttered a thank-you and plunged the serving spoon into the dish.

A half hour later, James sat on the couch with Fern as the boys cleared the table. Justin hadn't said much at dinner, answering James's questions tersely. He'd moved to Deerford with his mother and father two months ago. They had lived in Chicago his entire life. His favorite subject was art. That was about it. He hadn't looked James in the eye once.

"He seems like a nice boy," Fern said quietly.

James wasn't as sure and he wondered what the attraction was for Gideon. Most of his best friends were in JROTC or his advanced math and science classes. James put his arm around Fern and pulled her close to him. "Let's talk about Wednesday." Fern often teased him about his inclination to plan ahead, but he found it comforting to make sure all the bases were covered ahead of time.

"The appointment is at ten."

James nodded. He was taking the day off—much of his vacation time went to taking Fern to doctors' appointments. "We should leave before eight then." He preferred getting the boys out the door in the morning before they left for appointments. On weekday mornings once he left for work, Fern was home to see them out the door. It wasn't that he didn't think they would get to school on their own; it was that he thought it was good for kids to have someone around in the morning as they got ready for the day.

At nine o'clock James shuffled up the hardwood stairs to the second floor. The torrential rain had started again and was pelting the landing window.

James knocked on Gideon's door. "Son," he said. James didn't recognize the music but it was loud. "Son," he said again.

A moment later Gideon swung open the door.

"It's time for Justin to go home." James peered into the room. Justin sat at Gideon's desk, twirling a CD on his finger. He stood and lifted his sweatshirt from the back of the chair. His long hair had fallen across his face and James could see only one of the boy's eyes.

Gideon and Justin followed James down the stairs. "I'll bring my sketches to school tomorrow," Justin said as they reached the living room.

"Cool," Gideon answered, walking his friend to the front door.

James expected Justin to take out his cell and call or text for a ride but he didn't. "Do you need to borrow a phone?" he asked, standing in the middle of the room.

Justin shook his head. "I'm walking." He opened the door to the pounding of the rain on the street.

"Where do you live?" James took a few steps toward the boys.

"Out by the highway. Past the hospital."

"Close the door," James said. "I'll give you a ride." Fern was already tucked into bed and Nelson was finishing his homework. It wouldn't take long to drive Justin home.

"I can do it," Gideon said.

"Not tonight. It's too stormy." James opened the closet and pulled out his rain jacket. The storm was part of the reason—but honestly he was worried about Justin's influence too. He wasn't going to allow Gideon to drive Justin anywhere until James had a chance to get to know the boy better. "Get ready for bed," James called to Nelson as he pushed his arms through the sleeves of his jacket. "If Mom gets up, tell her I'll be right back."

James clicked the unlock button on the key fob as he ran to the van. Gideon and Justin followed, their heads tucked down against the storm.

"I've never seen so much rain," Justin said as he slammed the side door.

"It doesn't rain in Chicago?" James asked.

"Not like this."

"What brought your family to Deerford?" James hoped for more information from Justin about his family.

"My mom wanted to try it out," he said. "My grandma and grandpa live in Princeton. She wanted to be closer to them, but . . ." His voice trailed off.

James glanced in the rearview mirror. Justin was looking out the window, into the dark night.

As they rode along silently for a few minutes, Gideon turned the radio to the oldies station and James hummed along. They passed Deerford Park and then turned left toward the town square. Several minutes later, a few blocks east of Hope Haven, he stopped at the highway.

As James waited for a string of cars, their headlights blurred by the rain, Justin said, "I can walk from here."

"Afraid not." James turned quickly onto the highway. "I'm delivering you to your door on this dark and stormy night."

Besides being a long walk, it would have been a dangerous one by the time he reached the highway. James accelerated. "What's the next turn?" he asked.

"The next right. Our house is the second one on the left."

James followed the directions and stopped across the street from the house. Not a single light was on, not even the porch light. "Is anyone home?" James asked.

"My mom goes to bed early," he said. "And my dad is in Chicago." Justin hesitated and then added, "On business." He opened the door. "Thank you—for dinner and the ride."

The young man crossed the street and then headed up the walkway to the house. James was sure he saw Justin open the door but it was hard to be certain in the darkness. He pulled the car around in the street, hoping the lights would illuminate the porch. They did, but Justin either wasn't there or had already gone inside.

"What's his story?" James asked as he turned back onto the highway.

"What do you mean?" There was an edge to Gideon's voice.

"He seems sort of mysterious."

Gideon didn't answer.

"Son?"

Gideon crossed his arms. "You and Mom have always told us to be nice to new kids. I don't remember you ever saying we were supposed to judge them."

"Gid," James said, his voice soft. "I'm not judging Justin. I just want to know more about him."

They rode in silence, except for the seventies music and the drum of the rain on the roof of the van, the rest of the way home.

Chapter Three

AFTER HITTING END ON THE HOUSE PHONE, Anabelle put it back in its cradle. It was the third time she'd tried to call Ainslee. Chances were that she was at work. Anabelle opened the door off the kitchen and stepped onto the patio. Yesterday's storm had given way to a bright blue sky, and, thankfully, she had the day off due to comp time she needed to use.

The white blossoms on the cherry tree in the corner of the yard glittered like confetti in the sunshine and one of the cats ran out of the open barn door. Sarge barked, and the cat ran back in. Anabelle stepped down the terraced steps, careful not to slip on the wet wood, and followed the stone pathway Cameron had laid so carefully years ago across the yard.

Sarge hurried to her side, nuzzling her hand with his nose, his tail whipping around in a frenzy of delight. She stopped and rubbed his brown and white head and then continued along the path, past the red and yellow tulips and the blooming forsythia.

As she unlatched the back gate, commanding Sarge to stay, she could hear Cameron whistling in the barn through the half-open door.

The tabby cat rubbed against her leg as she slipped inside. It took a moment for her eyes to adjust to the dim light. The cat meowed and Anabelle stooped down, picked her up, and rubbed her neck. One of the other barn cats had delivered a litter of kittens a few days before, but Anabelle didn't have time to check on them now.

"Cameron?" she called out, squinting toward the back of the barn.

"Back here in the tool room."

A starling flew overhead, down from the open rafters, and the tabby squirmed and jumped to the swept cement floor. Anabelle stepped into the tool room. Cameron turned toward her, a pair of pruners in one hand and a sharpener in the other. Over the years, the extra tools from his landscaping service had retired to their barn. Now that Evan had taken over the business, Cameron had decided to refurbish the tools and either use them, sell them, or donate them.

"How's it going?" Anabelle asked.

"Good." He peered at her over his reading glasses, his blue eyes bright under his shock of gray hair. "What are you up to?"

"I thought I'd go into town."

"Annie—"

"To do the grocery shopping."

"And?"

"And yes I might stop by Once Upon A Time, but only because Barbara's birthday is coming up and she loves old things."

Cameron put the sharpening stone onto his bench and picked up an oilcan. "I thought you were going to give it a day or two."

"I can't."

He turned back toward her. "Or won't." He smiled gently. Anabelle had called Ainslee several times the previous night. Finally, on the fifth call, Ainslee had picked up, but seemed out of sorts. She'd hedged about whether she'd gone into work or not, but she did say she hadn't gotten a nap. That was why Anabelle had kept calling this morning—to see if her daughter was feeling better. It wasn't that she was worried about her health, after all it had been indigestion, but she was concerned Ainslee was going to become exhausted.

Anabelle straightened a rake that was crooked against the wall. "I'll just shop. I won't even ask how she's feeling," she said. "Did you call her? After we talked?"

Cameron shook his head. After she had shared about Ainslee being in the ER and then their conversation in the cafeteria, Cameron had been quiet. When she pressed him for his opinion he said he thought Ainslee needed some space. Anabelle agreed—after all that was what Elena had said too—so she suggested Cameron call their daughter to see how she was feeling. Obviously he hadn't.

"Well, do you need anything from the store?" Anabelle pushed up the sleeves of her sweater. Cameron had the space heater on, and the room was warm.

"I need more spray paint." He pointed to a can on his bench. "Black."

Anabelle stepped closer.

"Glossy. I'm going to spray the handles of the rakes and shovels."

She nodded as Cameron reached forward and kissed her on the lips. "I'll be back in time for lunch," she called out over her shoulder as she headed through the door.

"Annie." Cameron followed her. "Be gentle," he said.

She waved her hand dismissively. "I'm not going to say a thing—really. I'm just going to shop." She hurried out the barn door and back into the bright sunshine. Last night, as she and Cameron talked about Ainslee, Anabelle had resolved to step back, but the more she thought about it today the less certain she was. Ainslee had been sleep deprived yesterday, besides being hormonal. After a good night's sleep, she was bound to see things differently.

Anabelle stopped at the hardware store first and headed down the spray-paint aisle.

"May I help you?"

She turned around and came face-to-face with Larry Baxter, the owner of Baxter's Wares. "Oh, Anabelle," he said. "It's you." He crossed his thin arms. "What can I help you with?"

"I need a can of black spray paint. Glossy."

He squatted down, scanned the selection, and pulled a can from the bottom shelf. "We've had some problems with our spray paint—kids stealing it, that sort of thing," he said as he stood.

"Oh dear," Anabelle said. "Vandals hit the hospital the night before last." She'd been so caught up with Ainslee's ER visit that she hadn't sought out Eddie to see if the police had found the perpetrator.

"I know. The police tracked the paint to my store."

She shook her head in alarm. "Have they figured out who's responsible?"

Larry shook his head, a distressed expression on his face.

Anabelle stepped forward and patted his arm. "Well, you're not to blame."

The wrinkles on his high forehead, extended by his receding hairline, lifted. "They've asked me to keep track of who buys the paint."

Anabelle took a can off the shelf. "Cameron is sprucing up his tools." She smiled, feeling a little guilty even though she knew she had no reason to.

Larry nodded. "I'm tempted to stop carrying spray paint except I know that trustworthy people—like Cameron—use it too."

"The police will figure it out," Anabelle said. "And you're doing your best to help them. That's what counts." The vandal was affecting more people in the community than he probably realized.

After she'd checked out, she put the bag on the passenger seat of her car and then made sure the door was locked, hoping no one would be tempted to steal the paint. She chuckled to herself. It was in a paper sack; no one could tell what it was. She walked slowly down the sidewalk, admiring the winter pansies still in bloom in the cement planters. Surprisingly, yesterday's rain hadn't damaged them. She sighed. Maybe the storm had contributed to Ainslee's bad mood too.

Today was definitely a new day.

Anabelle pushed open the door to Once Upon A Time and stepped inside, peering over the racks of vintage clothes all the way to the back wall, looking for Ainslee, but she wasn't anywhere in sight. No one was. A rack of aprons caught Anabelle's eye. There were quilters who would snatch them up and turn them into quilts. It wasn't something Anabelle would do though. She lifted the skirt of a blue gingham apron. Her grandmother had worn a similar one years ago. Anabelle wondered what had happened to her grandmother's and mother's collections. She had a few of their old tea towels and tablecloths tucked away, but it would be nice to have the aprons for Ainslee and Kirstie although they probably wouldn't wear them.

A group of tin boxes caught her attention next. There was an English tea box, several old spice boxes, and a baking soda box. Next to these was a wooden box with a fleur-de-lis carved into the top. She picked it up. It was a hardwood, probably oak. The inside of the box was clean and smooth. She flipped it over. Twenty dollars. That was more than she usually spent on a co-worker's gift.

"Oh, hello, Anabelle." Minnie Webster, Ainslee's boss, poked her head around a shelf covered with toys from the 1960s—a Slinky, an Etch A Sketch, and a game of Twister. "Are you finding what you need?" Minnie wore a velvet bolero over a white blouse with ruffled sleeves and a long skirt. She was probably close to fifty but looked more like thirty-five with her bleached hair and bright makeup.

Anabelle held the box up. "I'm trying to make a decision about this. For a co-worker."

"I don't have any exact details on it except that it came from an estate sale in Springfield. A woman in her nineties. It was probably a handmade gift."

Anabelle nodded. "That's what I was thinking." She turned the box over again, hoping for a name or initials but there was nothing. Barbara was a romantic at heart. She would probably love the box. "I'll take it," she said, stepping around the toy shelf toward the counter. Perhaps Ainslee had called in sick today.

As she approached the counter she made a conscious effort to sound nonchalant. "Are you all by yourself today?"

"Oh no, Ainslee's in the back cleaning up some pottery." Minnie wrapped her fingers around the chain of the owl pendant around her neck. "I'll tell her you're here."

Anabelle started to say, "Oh, that's—" but Minnie had already stepped toward the curtain over the doorway and was calling out, "Ainslee, your mother's here."

Anabelle put her debit card on the counter and Minnie completed the transaction. "I thought maybe she'd stayed home to rest," Anabelle said. "After yesterday."

"Yesterday?" Minnie slipped the box into a paper bag.

Anabelle thought her voice was low, that there was no way Ainslee could hear her, but as her daughter came through the doorway, batting at the curtain, it was obvious she had.

"Mother," she said. She had on yellow rubber gloves and a yellow apron over her maternity top and pants.

"You're not using a solvent on that pottery, are you?" The words flew out of Anabelle's mouth.

"Soap and water," she said, practically glaring.

Minnie handed Anabelle her receipt and said, "It's so nice to see you. I have a few things to take care of"—she had a look of discomfort on her face—"in the back."

Anabelle wondered, as she clutched both the bag and the receipt in one hand, how much Ainslee had told Minnie. "So you did come into work yesterday."

Ainslee nodded. "I told you I was fine, but I don't appreciate your talking about my personal business with other people—especially my boss."

Anabelle put up her hand. "It slipped out. Honestly."

"I don't talk with everyone about everything the way you do, Mother."

Anabelle was aware of her head bobbing up and down. It wasn't that she was agreeing with Ainslee, not exactly. She didn't tell everyone everything. That was definitely an exaggeration. But she hoped her seeming agreement would soothe her daughter.

"I came into work yesterday afternoon. I already told you I didn't go home and take a nap." Ainslee gripped the edge of the counter. "I can make my own decisions."

"I'm sorry." Anabelle took a step backward, clutching her bag. "I'll do a better job respecting your privacy—I promise."

Ainslee crossed her arms. "You don't get it, do you?"

"Get what?"

"How your comments and phone calls make me feel."

"Sweetie." Anabelle wanted to take her daughter in her arms, but she knew that was definitely the wrong thing to do. "I'm just concerned about you, that's all. How about if you and Doug come to dinner tonight? We can talk then."

"We have our birth class tonight. We're working on a plan." Ainslee rested her hands atop her belly. "We're supposed to think about whom we want with us during labor."

Anabelle smiled, thankful that Ainslee had changed the subject. "You don't need to worry about that. Doug and I will be with you through the whole thing." It was something she'd looked forward to for years.

Ainslee crossed her arms and shook her head. "Actually, Mother, I'm not so sure."

Anabelle almost said, *You're not sure about Doug being there?* But then what her daughter was implying started to sink in and she whispered, "You don't mean—"

"Mother, I want this to be as stress-free as possible, and your criticizing me stresses me out. That's all."

Anabelle blinked and then said, "Ains, you have time to figure out a birth plan. You don't have to make a decision right now." Anabelle took another step backward.

"Please, Mother. Don't do that." Ainslee's voice held a hint of sympathy.

Anabelle's heart skipped a beat.

Ainslee kept speaking, her words coming like machine-gun fire now. "This is about what the baby and I need." Her voice was high and loud and she didn't sound like herself at all. "Right now, I need to get back to work. Thank you for understanding." Then she disappeared behind the curtain.

Thank you for understanding? Anabelle didn't understand any of it—not one word of what Ainslee had just said.

"I don't get it," Cameron said as he walked beside Anabelle to the end of Rishell Street. They turned right onto the dirt country lane and stayed toward the edge, away from the ruts of mud. Sarge ran ahead, off his leash.

Anabelle inhaled deeply and let it out slowly.

"You shouldn't take it personally that Ainslee might not want you at the birth." Cameron reached for her.

"How else would I take it?"

He squeezed her hand. "She doesn't want me there either."

"Cam." She leaned toward him as they walked, amused at his effort to comfort her. "Don't be ridiculous."

"And she hasn't asked Kirstie. Right? Or anyone else we know of—except Doug."

Anabelle nodded.

"And that's how it should be. That's how we want it. For her to depend on him the most."

"Well, sure, but a woman needs other women with her when she gives birth. Most of all, a woman needs her mother." Anabelle pulled her hand away and slipped it into the pocket of her jacket, along with Sarge's leash. She should have worn gloves.

"She'll have a labor and delivery nurse with her." Cameron led the way around a puddle.

Anabelle shoved her hands deeper into her pockets. Ainslee specifically wanted Candace at the birth, which was a relief to Anabelle because Candace was the best labor and delivery nurse at Hope Haven. And yes, she was mostly concerned about the safety of her daughter and grandchild-to-be, but she also wanted to be at the birth. Was there anything wrong with that?

The wind stirred up, rustling the bare branches over their heads that in the late spring, summer, and early fall were thickly covered with leaves, creating a tunnel through the trees. Today the treetops were bare, except for the beginnings of green buds taking hold—a mere indication of what was to come.

"Annie," Cameron said. "This will work out. Give it time."

Anabelle used to think that once all three of her children graduated high school, parenting would get easier. Then she set her sights on college graduation. In the everyday things, parenting was easier, but the things that did come up were more emotional and more trying than they used to be. How many times had she heard people say, "Bigger kids, bigger problems"? She swiped at her eyes with her icy hand. Cameron was right. This wasn't even a problem—except for her. The baby was fine. Ainslee was fine. The only person hurt was Anabelle.

"She needs to be in control of her own life," Cameron said. "Especially now." He smiled at her. "Remember how your mom used to drive you nuts?"

"That was different."

Cameron didn't respond.

"Her advice was ridiculous. Don't you remember? She wanted to dip Evan's pacifier in honey to get him to take it. She could have given him botulism if I hadn't been there. And she thought iceberg lettuce was nutritious. And she would have fed the kids candy every chance she had if I hadn't put my foot down."

Cameron was shaking his head. "You're right—it was different. Still, the feelings were probably the same."

Suddenly Anabelle wasn't as cold as she had been. "What are you getting at?"

Cameron shook his head. "Nothing."

"I am *not* like my mother."

"I didn't say you were."

"I'm a nurse—I know what Ainslee and her baby need."

Cameron reached for her hand. "I know, Annie. My point was that young mothers need to be able to speak their minds. Just like you were able to with your mother."

Anabelle exhaled. "Oh." She'd overreacted.

"Maybe you've been working too hard," Cameron said. "Can you take some more time off? Get some extra rest?"

"I'm fine." *Sure, I work hard for someone my age, but that's what keeps me young. Besides, if I don't stay busy with work, I'll have even more time to think about Ainslee, and I definitely don't need that.* They walked in silence for a few minutes.

"Shall we turn back? Before it's dark?" Cameron's eyes were on the horizon to the west. He whistled for Sarge, and the dog came loping back toward them.

Anabelle pulled the leash from her pocket and clicked it onto the dog's collar. "How about a pot of soup? And cheese bread?"

They turned, avoiding a puddle that nearly spread across the entire lane. Ahead a sparrow fluttered off into the blackberry brambles along the fence line. Anabelle and the children used to pick the berries and make cobbler in the summer. In a few more years, she and her grandchild would be able to do that. If Ainslee would allow it.

Chapter Four

"COME ON, HOWIE." CANDACE STOOD IN THE DOORWAY of her son's room. "We need to go."

He dropped his Star Wars fighter onto his bed and spun around, tripping over his own foot and sprawling out on the floor. He turned his face toward her, laughing, his green eyes shining.

Candace couldn't help but smile at him. He was her sunshine. "Get your coat and backpack. We need to leave." She started down the hall, slinging her purse over her shoulder. Brooke had left a half hour ago, saying she needed help with her math assignment. It seemed the homework in sixth grade increased as each week of school marched by. Thankfully her daughter kept up with the load.

Howie's footsteps came up behind her. "'Scuse me!" he yelled, barreling past her.

"Sweetie." Candace planted her hand on his shoulder. "Slow down. We don't run in the house."

"But we're late," he said, twisting away from her, his thick copper hair brushing against her arm.

"We're never too late not to use good manners. Now *walk* to the entryway and put your coat on." She let go of him and he lunged forward, falling on the carpet and then jumping back to his feet. Everything seemed to be a game to him.

Candace stepped into the kitchen. Her mother sat at the table, going through the newspaper ads.

"I'm going to run a few errands after I talk to Mrs. Gray," Candace said. "Do you need anything?"

Janet shook her head. "I'll get groceries this afternoon. There are some good specials." She pointed to the ad in front of her. "Whole fryers are just eighty-nine cents a pound. And lean hamburger is only two seventy."

"Great, I'll make meatloaf tonight." Candace waved to her mother and pulled her driving gloves out of her pocket, slipping them onto her hands as she stepped into the entryway.

Howie sat in the middle with his backpack open in front of him, his hand inside. He jumped when he saw Candace, and she bent down beside him.

"Howie," she said, pulling his fighter out of his bag. "You know we don't take toys to school."

"But I want to." Howie wiggled away.

"Put this back in your room." Candace stood and handed it to him.

He frowned but started down the hallway. Candace sighed and decided to follow. If she left him on his own, he might start building a whole space station. Sure enough when she reached his bedroom, he was on the floor with bricks of Legos in both hands.

"Howie," she said, "we need to go. Now."

Ten minutes later Candace pulled her Honda CRV into the parking lot of Rishell Elementary School. Howie had his booster seat unfastened before she turned the motor off. "Whoa, buddy," she said. "Next time wait until I take the key out of the ignition."

He pulled on the handle of the door but the safety locks were on, just like they always were. Candace sighed as she opened her door, wondering what normal boy behavior was. She felt the pang of Dean's death. Howie was only two when his father died, just a toddler. When she thought of all the stages they had ahead of them, she felt a little overwhelmed. She knew nothing about boys. She made a mental note to discuss this with her colleague Heath Carlson at the hospital. He normally provided great insight and support when she needed it.

She opened Howie's door and took his hand. He grabbed his backpack with the other and jumped to the asphalt. He'd unzipped his down jacket and it flapped open as he landed.

"Let's race," Candace said, once they reached the sidewalk. Perhaps she could deplete some of this boundless energy so he wouldn't be a handful for his teacher.

Howie laughed as he took off running, his backpack bouncing on his shoulders. The playground lawn was just beginning to green, and the bricks of the school appeared brighter than usual in the morning sun. Candace stayed a step behind her son, catching up with him as he reached the front door, out of breath.

"Now," Candace said, kneeling on the cement and looking her son in the eye, "we use our inside voices and inside actions. Right?"

His head bobbed up and down. "Right." Mrs. Gray, the teacher who took over his class in January, had sent Candace an e-mail asking to meet with her but hadn't given a clue as to why.

Candace pushed open the wide wooden door to the school. "I'll talk with Mrs. Gray while you play quietly until the other students arrive. Then I'll leave."

Howie nodded as he led the way into the building. It was the quintessential century-old school with high ceilings, freshly painted hallways with a strip of accent molding, and polished linoleum floors. Artwork was displayed above the molding and murals were taped below.

"That's my painting," Howie said, pointing as they turned the corner.

Candace stopped. It was a drawing of a space station with a red ball behind it. "It's very nice, sweetie," she said.

"That's a planet," Howie explained. "It's about to get blown up."

"Oh." That was exactly the sort of thing that Candace didn't know how to respond to. They continued walking down the hall and then entered the classroom.

Howie's teacher sat at her nearly clear desk.

"Hello," Candace said, pulling off her gloves.

Mrs. Gray shook Candace's hand gracefully and turned her attention to Howie. "Please put your backpack and coat away and then choose a book in the reading corner." The woman wore her salt-and-pepper hair in a short, efficient style.

"Mama said I could play." Howie's demeanor had quickly turned from cheerful to sullen.

Candace's face reddened. "Please do what Mrs. Gray said."

Howie shuffled off to the row of hooks and cubbies.

"Take a seat, please." Mrs. Gray motioned to one of two grown-up sized chairs by a little table.

Candace sat and wiggled out of her wool coat, draping it over the back of the chair while Mrs. Gray picked up a file from her desk. The woman's face was full and barely wrinkled for her age, and her blue eyes had an expression of firmness. She sat down across from Candace and straightened the sleeves of her forest green sweater.

"Thank you for coming," Mrs. Gray said. "Howie is a charming boy. He's well liked by his classmates and I find him enjoyable too. He's very enthusiastic and eager to help."

Candace smiled. It always warmed her to hear nice things being said about her children.

Mrs. Gray smiled back and then said, "But—"

Candace's heart sank. Of course there was a reason for the meeting. It wasn't just for Mrs. Gray to praise Howie.

"Howie can also be disruptive. He frequently speaks loudly and out of turn, and I'll sometimes turn around to find him out of his chair. Last week, one of the other boys said Howie tripped him out on the playground. And just yesterday he interrupted our story time with an outburst of noises that sounded like gunfire." Mrs. Gray crossed her arms as she finished speaking.

"Oh dear." Candace leaned forward. Nothing like this had gone on with Mrs. Lambert, at least she didn't think it had.

"Have there been any changes at home? Anything that would have upset him?"

Candace shook her head.

"I see that he lives with you, his sister, and his grandmother." Mrs. Gray opened the file in front of her. "Is his father in the picture?"

Candace had explained all of this to Mrs. Lambert at the fall conference. "Howie's father—my husband—passed away almost four years ago."

"Oh dear." Mrs. Gray flipped through the documents in the file. "I had no idea, and I don't see any mention of that."

Candace exhaled slowly. "Most of the teachers here know—my daughter Brooke was a third grader at the time."

"How sad." Mrs. Gray's eyes were sympathetic. "Has anything happened recently that would stir any of this up for Howie?"

Candace shook her head. "No. Not at all. In fact, things have been pretty calm."

Mrs. Gray seemed to consider Candace's words for a moment and then she said, "Well, then I think we should consider testing."

"For?" Candace's heart rate was increasing.

"Attention deficit disorder. That sort of thing."

Candace swallowed hard. "I know he can be active, but he's a little boy. He doesn't seem any more active than his friends."

"It's not uncommon for boys this age to be busy, but Howie seems to have a very hard time focusing."

"Can you give me more examples—besides interrupting the story?"

Mrs. Gray pulled out a paper from the file. "Ah, here are my notes. He has a hard time sitting at his desk. In fact, half the time he stands to do his work."

"Mrs. Lambert was okay with that." They'd discussed it at the fall conference in fact.

"It's not something I'm comfortable with." Mrs. Gray met Candace's eyes. "How could I manage a class with twenty-seven kindergartners standing?"

Candace wanted to crawl under the table.

The teacher looked back down at her notes. "And multiple times he hasn't followed directions because he wasn't listening—or perhaps because he simply chose not to."

Candace nodded. "But is that unusual for this age?" A jolt of defensiveness caught Candace off guard. "It's just that he's still learning how to listen and take directions." Candace cringed, knowing she sounded as if she were making excuses, but Mrs. Gray didn't respond.

Instead she pulled a business card from another file. "I've been teaching for thirty years, and this doctor"—she passed the card across the table to Candace—"is the best in the area."

Candace read the name. Dr. Samuel Lloyd. The address was in Peoria. Candace was surprised that her voice came out a little shaky. "Do you think there are other things we can do? Like behavior modification? That sort of thing."

"You certainly can try." Mrs. Gray closed the file. "But take him to the doctor, dear. It could make a world of difference."

Candace turned and watched Howie for a moment. He was on his stomach, his feet toward her, moving his right leg up and down at the knee. Candace slipped the card into her jeans pocket.

"See," Mrs. Gray said. "He has such a hard time staying still."

Candace turned back and faced the teacher. "How common is"—she cleared her throat, finding it hard to say—"ADD?"

Mrs. Gray stood; her voice was soft. "Oh, I'm having this same type of meeting with three other parents. Howie's not alone. In a classroom of this size there are always several students who have it. It's a proven statistic, really."

"Oh." Candace stood too and slipped into her coat.

"Let me know what you find out," the teacher said. "And remember, the sooner you get him tested, the sooner we can come up with a solution."

"Thank you," Candace said, although she didn't feel like she meant it. The woman made her nervous.

Mrs. Gray took her hand. "We're in this together. You're Howie's most important advocate, and I'm his second."

Candace said that she would keep Mrs. Gray updated. Then she headed to the reading corner to tell Howie, who was now kicking both legs up and down, to have a good day.

He twisted to a squatting position as she approached, clutching the book to his chest.

"How's the book?" Candace asked.

Howie frowned. "I was just looking at the pictures. Mrs. Gray read it to us last week."

"And?" Candace kneeled beside him.

He opened the book. "It's about frogs. All kinds. Tree frogs. Rain forest frogs. Poison dart frogs. I'm going to ask if I can borrow it to take home."

"I'll read it to you," Candace said. She hugged him and said she would pick him up after school, that they would walk home together.

"Bye, Mommy," he said and then plopped down on the rug, his nose back in the book.

The morning bell rang as Candace stepped into the hall, and children began streaming through the front door in a parade of colorful jackets, scarves, and hats. Everyone looked so happy, as if they didn't have a care in the world. In the back of her mind, she had worried at times that Howie might be too active. Her throat constricted as she pulled on her gloves. But she never suspected he had ADD.

"You're back early." Candace's mother stood at the kitchen sink, wringing out the dishcloth.

"I'm going to run my errands later, before I pick up the kids." Candace put her keys and purse on the table. "I decided to work out first." She headed toward the hall. Every once in a while she traded her day off. Her usual day off was Thursday.

"Candace," Mom said. "Is something wrong? How did the meeting go with Mrs. Gray?"

"Okay." Candace wasn't ready to talk about it yet. She continued up the stairs and opened the door to her room. This was where she always came when she was distraught—it was her escape, the place where she felt, although dimly now, Dean's presence. Her eyes fell on her wedding photo on the far wall across the room, and she plopped down on her sleigh bed. Dean looked so handsome, his blond hair nearly white in the sunlight and his blue eyes lit up by his beautiful smile. The expression on his face, as he gazed at her, was of absolute abandon.

Next her eyes fell on the photo on her nightstand, the last photo she had of Dean with the children. Eight-year-old Brooke wore a pale pink Easter dress with a tulle skirt, and she gripped her basket with both hands. Two-year-old Howie wore a little blue suit and swung his basket at his side with one hand and held Dean's hand with his other. His eyes were scrunched up in a full-face smile.

Tears filled her eyes and she swiped them away. She was overreacting, she was sure. Howie might have ADD. But it wasn't life and death. They'd already faced so many things that had been much harder, including Brooke's inability to talk for months after Dean's death.

Maybe it wasn't the possibility of ADD that she was reacting to. Maybe it was the isolation she felt, the fact that she was in this all alone. Sure, her mother was there, helping her every step of the way, but it wasn't the same. She couldn't talk this sort of thing through with Janet the way she could have with Dean. She didn't have a man's perspective, and she didn't have any experience with little boys. She had raised two girls, Candace and her sister, Susan. In fact, no one else in the family had boys, which made Howie an anomaly.

She dug out the doctor's card from her jeans pocket. If he said Howie had ADD, she would have to decide, on her own, what to do. She shivered.

As she pulled sweatpants and a long-sleeved T-shirt from her drawer, her mother knocked on her door. "I decided to go do the grocery shopping now. Is there anything else we need? Besides what you already said?"

"No. Thanks, Mom." Candace unfurled her workout pants and began changing out of her jeans.

"Are you sure you're okay, dear?" Her mother's voice was muffled through the door.

"I'm fine—just changing my clothes." Candace tried to make her voice lighter, cheerier. "I'll see you when you get back from shopping."

"I'm going to have lunch with Susan. How about if you join us?"

Candace pulled her shirt over her head. She didn't feel like she would be very good company.

"Come on, sweetheart. You have plenty of time to work out and then change."

"Maybe," Candace said. She didn't want to talk about Howie and the meeting with Mrs. Gray with her mom and sister, not yet.

"Well, you don't need to decide now. You can let me know later."

"Okay. Thanks, Mom." Candace pulled her athletic shoes out from under the bed and put them on, lacing them up tight. She pulled her gym bag from the closet and grabbed a towel from her bathroom. A hard workout would do her good. Maybe nothing was wrong with Howie—maybe he was just an average boy. He'd been her snuggle bug for the last four years, the one who brought her the most comfort. Because he couldn't remember Dean, she hadn't worried about him as much. And he'd never given her any reason to worry.

He was a happy kid who seemed both secure and content. Sure he was active, but it hadn't seemed overwhelming to her, not really. She ground her teeth together. Now she was thinking in circles. She grabbed the doctor's card and stuffed it into the pocket of her jacket.

Candace wiped the sweat from her forehead with her towel as she sat in her car in the parking garage of the gym. She'd gone fifty minutes on the treadmill, ten minutes longer than usual, and had gone through her weight-lifting circuit twice. She started the car and then patted the pocket of her jacket, feeling the doctor's card. There was nothing like a good workout to make her more optimistic.

She pulled her cell phone from her purse and dialed the number. The receptionist barely said hello before putting her on hold. Shadows jumped around in the dim light of the garage as she listened to instrumental music that she didn't recognize and watched gym members hurry by, some dashing toward the gym, others lumbering toward their cars.

The receptionist came back on the line. "Thank you for waiting."

Candace explained the reason for her call.

"We're currently booked for the next three weeks," the receptionist said, "although I can put you on the list for a cancellation."

"Please do," Candace said and then made the appointment. She didn't want to wait four weeks to get the doctor's opinion; she wanted to know what they were dealing with now. She hung up the phone. It was ten thirty. She would go home and get a load of laundry started, jump in the shower, and help Janet put away the groceries. Maybe she would even go out to lunch with her mother and her sister Susan. She was definitely feeling better.

Two hours later she sat in the Parlor Restaurant listening to Susan talk about how her daughter Sarah was doing in her sophomore honors classes at Lincoln High School. "Still straight A's," Susan said. "Not that I'm bragging." She smiled.

"It's not bragging," Janet said. "It's sharing." She smiled, her forehead lifting up to her all-white hair. "Besides we're family.

This is the place to let it all hang out." She turned the handle of her coffee cup to the side. "Speaking of . . . Candace, how about some details about that meeting with Howie's teacher?"

Candace braced herself. "There's not much to tell."

"Is something wrong?" Susan asked.

Candace shook her head. "The teacher wanted to touch base. She's new."

Susan pursed her lips and glanced at her sister. She stirred her coffee, her two gold bracelets jingling together as she did. "I've been debating whether to say anything or not." She cocked her head to the side, brushing her stylish cut from her eyes. "But maybe I should." She smiled. "I've noticed Howie seems more active lately, you know, jumping around, poking at Brooke, that sort of thing. Sarah mentioned it too."

Candace felt her face freeze. They'd all had dinner together on Saturday and Howie had been wound up, but it had been raining for days and he hadn't been outside. She'd attributed it to cabin fever.

Susan leaned forward. "You would not believe how out of control boys are these days." She was practically whispering. "When Sarah was in middle school, the boys just could not sit still. It's amazing they learned anything at all. That's why it's such a relief to have her in the honors classes."

"But Howie's in kindergarten," Candace said. "Don't you think being active is normal?" Maybe kindergartners and middle schoolers had a lot in common.

Janet cleared her throat. "Most boys are active." She probably felt like she needed to be the peacemaker. "But does his teacher feel like he's within the range of normal?"

Candace wrinkled her nose. "Mrs. Lambert did."

"What about Mrs. Gray?"

Candace sighed. *I might as well tell them.* "She thinks I should take him to a specialist."

"Well, there you go," Susan said.

Candace ignored her sister.

"Do you have someone in mind, dear?" Janet's eyes were kind.

Candace nodded. "Mrs. Gray gave me a name. Howie has an appointment in several weeks."

"Several weeks?" Susan said. "He'll be nearly done with kindergarten by then."

"It was the first available appointment," Candace said, feeling defeated. As she spoke, the waitress approached. Candace's mind wandered as her sister and mother ordered. Maybe she hadn't been demanding enough of Howie, and he was simply behaving badly. She thought she'd been so careful not to baby him, but maybe she had, inadvertently.

"And for you?" the waitress said.

"Oh." Candace glanced back down at the menu. "The soup and salad special please, with the house vinaigrette on the side."

"So," Janet said, as the waitress left, "let me tell you about the peonies I'm looking to buy. They'll look perfect in the backyard. Do you remember the peonies we had . . ."

Candace appreciated her mother's changing the subject, but she was having a hard time following the conversation. She took a sip of water and gazed out the window. A father and preschool-aged son ran by, the boy leading the way. He looked over his shoulder and his dad sped up, scooping the boy up into a bear hug.

"Candace?" Susan was peering at her. "You okay?" her sister asked.

She nodded. But she wasn't, not at all. She felt icy cold. The waitress was headed toward them with Candace's soup, but she knew its warmth would do nothing to melt the familiar loneliness inside of her.

Chapter Five

ARBARA SAT IN HER SWIVEL CHAIR AT THE nurses' station and held the carved box in her hand. "It's beautiful." She stood, putting the wrapping paper on the desk, and hugged Anabelle. "Where in the world did you find it?"

"Once Upon A Time," Anabelle answered, letting go of her friend.

The phone rang. "Excuse me." Barbara sat back down in her chair and answered the call.

Anabelle turned her attention to the computer, with one ear to Barbara's conversation. It was obvious that a new admit was on the way. There was a pause in the conversation and Barbara turned to Anabelle. "Forty-four-year-old woman. Heart attack."

"Oh dear."

Barbara held up her index finger and turned her attention back to the phone. "Yes, I'm still here. Okay, we'll expect her ASAP." Barbara hung up the phone. "She's on her way."

Anabelle turned toward the dry-erase board with the assign-ments. "I guess I'd better take her. We'll put her in bed seven." It was the only one left. "I'll go get the room ready." She hurried down the hall. Forty-four was young for a heart attack. Thank-fully the woman had gotten to the ER in time—often heart attacks in women were misdiagnosed.

Anabelle hurried into room 207 and readied the nitro drip. More women were having heart attacks because they had more stressful jobs than in the past, or so they said. Anabelle was sure that being a mother was the hardest job of all, so it didn't entirely make sense to her. But maybe the satisfaction of motherhood, in the long run, countered the stress.

She turned down the bed and then began putting stickers on the heart electrodes, preparing them to put on the patient. Women sometimes had back or stomach pain when they were having cardiac symptoms instead of the shooting arm pain so common in men. Sometimes docs totally missed that women were having heart attacks.

Anabelle positioned the heart monitor and then stepped out of the room into the hall. The elevator door opened and the gurney appeared. She waved to the transportation aide. "In here," she said, motioning, and then asked, "Where's the ER nurse?" A nurse always accompanied the transfers.

"She was too busy," the young man said.

The patient turned her head toward Anabelle. She had long dark hair, spread over the pillow, and she looked small and helpless on the gurney. The aide and Anabelle worked together and transferred the patient onto the bed. Anabelle covered her up with the sheet and two cotton thermal blankets and then took the clipboard from the head of the gurney. Marcia Barnes was the woman's name.

"Hello, Marcia," she said. "I'm your nurse, Anabelle."

Marcia grimaced.

"How bad is your pain?" Anabelle asked, turning to the computer to check the chart to see when she was last given a pain med.

"About a seven," the woman answered, grimacing again.

According to the chart, she'd been given morphine three hours ago. It was definitely time for some more. Anabelle read further. The EKG indicated it was an anterior MI, on the front side of her heart.

Anabelle turned back to Marcia. "I'll go get some more pain medication for you." She started to leave but stopped at the end of the bed. "Did anyone come to the hospital with you?"

"My son did, but he went on to school." Marcia's voice was low. "My husband is in Chicago—looking for a job. We haven't been able to get hold of him." Marcia's brown eyes watered.

Anabelle took a closer look. She was sure she didn't recognize her. "How long have you lived in Deerford?"

"A couple months."

A new town. A husband away job hunting. And now a heart attack. "How old is your son?"

"He's a freshman at the high school. He's the one who called the paramedics during the night—he had to use the neighbors' phone. And then he stayed with me in the ER. But we thought he should go ahead and go to class."

"Oh." He sounded like an exceptional kid. "I'll be right back," Anabelle said and headed out the door to the med station.

THE HEART OF THE MATTER • 55

She should sneak away and talk to Pastor Tom before her shift was over. He needed to know about Marcia and her family.

After Anabelle added the morphine to Marcia's IV drip, the woman slept, giving Anabelle time to read the rest of her chart. The ER doc had put in an order for an angiogram, so there was prep work to do for that. Also, not all of Marcia's lab work had come back, so Anabelle would need to keep checking for that too. In the meantime, she needed to do the assignments for swing shift and work on the long-term schedule for the unit.

When she checked on Marcia again, the woman was awake, trying to straighten out the sheets and blankets that were in a tumble around her legs. "Let me do it," Anabelle said, but as she untwisted the bedding, she noticed a purple mark on the woman's thigh. "That's quite the bruise," she said, trying to hide her alarm. "How'd you get it?"

"I bumped into our table—it has a sharp edge." Marcia's voice was barely a whisper. She winced as she finished speaking.

Anabelle took a closer look. It appeared to be about a week old. She pulled up the sheet and noticed a mark at the sleeve line of Marcia's hospital gown. "What's this?" Anabelle pushed up the sleeve. The bruise spread all the way to her shoulder.

Marcia wiggled away from Anabelle's hand. "I'm pretty clumsy—I fell against the car mirror." Again, her voice was low and hard to hear.

Anabelle tried to imagine the scenario but couldn't work it out in her mind. Her instincts told her there was more to the story than clumsiness. Maybe Marcia's husband was in Chicago for more reasons than looking for a job. It was better to be safe and report it to the on-staff social worker. Surely the ER nurse had seen the bruises—Anabelle needed to check to see if they'd already been reported even though they hadn't been included in her chart.

At the nurse's station, Anabelle called down to the ER and asked to speak with the nurse who had admitted Marcia, but she was on break. "Please have her call me as soon as she gets back," Anabelle said. "It's urgent."

As she headed toward Marcia's room, a young man slipped through the door ahead of her. She quickened her step. "May I help you?" she said as she entered the room.

He was just a boy really, wearing a black sweatshirt with the hood pulled tight on his head. "My mom," he said, motioning to Marcia. The woman was sleeping again.

"She needs to rest," Anabelle said. "Can you go get something to eat? And come back in about an hour?" The boy must have cut class to come back to the hospital.

He put his hand on the end of the bed for a moment, revealing long fingernails. He looked nothing like the young man Anabelle imagined when Marcia said her son had called 911 in the middle of the night and escorted her to the hospital.

Anabelle kept a pleasant expression on her face. "If she wakes up before you get back, I'll tell her to expect you soon."

The boy grunted and darted out the door.

Anabelle checked Marcia's blood pressure and pulse on the monitor and then opened her chart again. The angio was scheduled for three o'clock. Anabelle studied the sleeping woman. Dark circles shadowed her eyes and she seemed too thin. Anabelle couldn't help but wonder what her story was.

As Anabelle approached the nurse's desk, Barbara stood, her hand against the receiver of the phone. "It's for you," she said. "It's the ER nurse."

Anabelle picked up the other phone and explained the reason for her call.

"I was pretty busy when she came in," the nurse said. It wasn't anyone whose name Anabelle recognized. "I didn't really notice any bruises." The woman sounded young.

"They're pretty obvious," Anabelle said. "On her leg, and the one on her arm looks as if someone gripped her really hard."

"Maybe the lighting down here is bad," the woman said.

Anabelle lowered her voice. "How long have you been working at Hope Haven? I don't think we've met."

"I'm an agency nurse."

"Oh." Anabelle paused. "Well, thank you for your help." Now she needed to report both the bruises and the nurse. She hung up the phone. And she needed to talk to Pastor Tom. She hadn't taken a break—a quick run downstairs would do her good.

"I'll be right back," Anabelle said to Barbara, stepping away from the nurses' desk. She hurried down the steps to the first floor, hurrying past the chapel and on down to the Social Services Department. Janice Thompson's office door was open slightly and she sat at her desk on the phone.

"Just a minute," she mouthed. She was a thin, tall woman in her midthirties with long brown hair, parted on the side.

Anabelle stood in front of the bulletin board. There were brochures from Meals on Wheels, Big Brothers Big Sisters, Veterans Affairs, Bureau County Health, Child and Protective

Services, Drug and Alcohol Treatment, and Heating Assistance. Anabelle was so thankful for Janice and the other social workers and their expertise. It was such a relief to be able to pass on any suspicious circumstances to them.

"Come on in." Janice's voice was kind. "What can I do for you?"

Anabelle explained Marcia's bruises, and Janice accessed her file on the computer. "I see you already charted it," she said. "Good. I'll go speak with her before I go home." She smiled.

"Thank you," Anabelle said, knowing Janice would then report it to Protective Services. "Her husband is in Chicago looking for a job. It's my understanding that their son hasn't been able to reach him."

"Oh? And how old is the son?"

"A teenager, maybe fifteen."

Janice jotted down a few notes on the pad on her desk. "Thanks, Anabelle. All of this information is helpful."

On her way to the stairwell, Anabelle stepped into the chapel. Light from the fading afternoon sun streamed through the stained-glass window above the altar, casting hues of scarlet, purple, and emerald across the oak pews. She knocked on Pastor Tom's office door but no one answered. She would chat with him later.

When she returned to Marcia's room, the woman's son was sitting by her bed, his head in his hands. His hood hung down on his back, revealing long, stringy hair.

"Is she still asleep?" Anabelle asked even though she could see that Marcia was.

The boy nodded.

"I'm Anabelle." She extended her hand. "I should have introduced myself before."

"Justin." He limply shook her hand.

"Did you get something to eat?" Anabelle kept her voice low. He shrugged.

"Did you leave school early?" she asked.

"I couldn't concentrate," he answered.

"Your mom's scheduled for an angiogram at three to assess the blockage in her heart. I'm not sure how long it will take."

He didn't respond, and Anabelle left the room to finish the evening-shift assignments. When she returned fifteen minutes later, Marcia was speaking softly. "Call them," she said. "From here." She nodded to the phone beside her bed.

Justin shook his head.

"Sweetie." Marcia's eyes pled with him.

"I'll stay with my buddy," Justin said. "He's from a good family."

Marcia closed her eyes.

"Can I help with something?" Anabelle felt bad she hadn't offered before and didn't think to mention it to Janice. It was obvious that with his father in Chicago and mother in the hospital that someone else needed to be responsible for Justin.

Justin stood. "No, I have things figured out. I'm going for a walk."

Anabelle searched Marcia's eyes.

"He's staying with a friend," Marcia said and then sighed. She reached for her son. "Come back later, okay?"

He squeezed her hand, bumping the end of the bed as he stepped toward the door. His face was drawn, and he gave Anabelle a cold look as he hurried out of the room.

A half hour later, as Anabelle checked Marcia's vital signs again, Janice breezed into the room, a cheery look on her face. She towered over the bed and as soon as she introduced herself, she sat down in the chair Justin had vacated, chatting with Marcia for several minutes, asking her questions that Anabelle knew the social worker already had the answers to. Janice was most likely doing her best to win Marcia's trust, but Marcia didn't seem to be cooperating. She was still tense and guarded and Anabelle couldn't tell if it was from the pain or something else.

Janice lowered her voice and her tone softened even more. "I've been told you have a couple of nasty bruises."

Marcia slumped down in the bed. "They're not bad. I'm so clumsy—I fell against our table several days ago and then against the car mirror."

"Was that before or after your husband went to Chicago?"

A puzzled look crossed Marcia's face. "Before." She paused. "No after." She shook her head a little and her eyes grew moist. "I fell against the car mirror before—because he took the car to Chicago." Her voice fell to a whisper. "But I fell against the table after he left."

Anabelle couldn't help but notice the woman's confusion.

"Mind if I take a look?" Janice leaned forward.

"I'm really tired," Marcia said. "Could you come back later?"

Janice stood. "It will only take a minute."

Marcia exhaled and then pushed the sleeve of her gown up for a split second. Then she quickly thrust her leg out from the blankets and shifted to her side. "See," she said. "You can see where I landed against the corner of the table. That's why the bruise is so dark in the middle." As she slipped her leg back under the covers, Janice jotted down a couple of notes. A moment later transportation arrived to take Marcia to the cath lab.

Janice stepped back to the corner of the room as Anabelle and the aide transferred Marcia to the gurney and then, as soon as they left the room, Anabelle turned toward the social worker and asked, "What do you think?"

"I think we have a problem." Janice's expression was one of pure concern.

It had been a long, hard day and a little late afternoon pick-me-up was exactly what Anabelle needed. A draft of cold air, as if someone had left the back door of the cafeteria open, assaulted her as she headed toward the coffee machines. She poked her head around the corner into the dining area and gasped. Eddie was picking up broken glass off a table and above him was a shattered window.

"Eddie," she called out. "What happened?"

"The Hope Haven vandal struck again—in broad daylight." He shook his head in disgust as he dropped a long shard of glass into a bucket. "He threw a rock right through the window— fortunately no one was in the dining room at the time."

"Oh dear." Anabelle bent to help him pick up glass.

"No, no—I don't want you getting cut," he said. She noted his leather gloves and stood. He was right.

"This has been the third time he's struck this week." Eddie's expression was filled with anger.

"What else besides the other morning?" Anabelle wrapped her arms around herself. She'd hoped that the vandalism the other morning was a one-time act.

"A second round of graffiti on the bricks near the ER door," Eddie answered. "Last night—in the middle of the night. It was there this morning when I came to work, but I got it cleaned up right away." He put the last of the large pieces into the bucket and turned toward the shop vac beside the table. "Let me know if you see anything suspicious," he said to Anabelle. "We need to stop this vandal."

"Absolutely," Anabelle said. "This is unacceptable in our community." Anabelle thanked Eddie for all his hard work, and headed back to the coffee machine, speculating about what kind of person would vandalize a place where the sick were cared for. It didn't make any sense. Hope Haven didn't have any enemies.

Chapter Six

JAMES SLOWED THE VAN AS THEY ENTERED THE CITY limits of Deerford, and Fern stirred in the passenger seat.

"Are we home?" Her voice was barely audible and her speech was slurred.

"Just about," James answered. She'd had a sedative for the MRI and had slept all the way home from Chicago. James yawned. It had been a long day.

Fern shifted her position, sat up straight, and tucked a strand of her wavy hair behind her ear. "Did we start anything for dinner before we left?"

"No," James said, a little alarmed that she couldn't remember. Sometimes they put a roast in the Crock-Pot but he hadn't had enough time this morning. Maybe they would have tomato soup and grilled cheese sandwiches for dinner tonight, something simple. James yawned again. He was completely spent. He hoped the boys had done their chores and started on their homework.

He didn't have the energy to play the part of a drill sergeant tonight.

"When will I find out about the MRI?" Fern asked.

James turned onto Sixth Avenue. "In a couple of days," he said. "The doctor will call." He'd asked him to call his cell phone though—he couldn't always rely on Fern to remember a phone conversation, especially if she'd been napping before she answered.

A minute later James turned onto McCleaf Street, and as he approached their house, Gideon stepped out into the street, an expression of alarm on his face. James's heart raced as he pushed the button for Fern's window.

"Justin's mom had a heart attack," Gideon said.

"I'm really sorry to hear that, Gid."

"He needs us to meet him there."

James felt for his son and his son's friend. There was nothing he could do at the hospital, though, that the nurses in Cardiac Care weren't already doing. Besides, he barely had the energy to care for his own family tonight, let alone someone else's.

"Dad." Gideon's voice was shrill.

"Gideon, I'll park. Then we'll talk. Meet me in the house." James raised the window and accelerated into the driveway.

"Poor woman," Fern said. "Imagine, a heart attack. She can't be very old."

He put the car into park and turned off the engine. Fern had her door open by the time he reached it and was swinging her legs around, her cane in her hand.

"Let me help," he said. He would carry her in the house if she would let him, but that would mortify her. He took her elbow and helped her stand.

"Oh dear," she said, slumping back down onto the seat, her hand flying up to her head.

"What is it?"

"My head. I feel like I've just been hit with a hammer."

"Dad." Gideon stood at the end of the driveway.

"Not now," James said. Gideon clomped up the front steps as James hovered over Fern. "Can you make it into the house?" he asked.

"I think so," she answered. "If we take it slow."

James put his arm around her. "Lean against me," he said, guiding her toward the back door where there were fewer steps. She'd had a new injection, and the doctor had warned that a headache might come on quickly. James was relieved to know it was normal.

Nelson, in his stockinged feet, held the back door open; Fern reached out and patted his shoulder but didn't try to speak.

"Mom's feeling pretty bad," James said to his son. "She got a shot that should help her feel better, but it's given her a horrific headache."

Nelson nodded solemnly and then closed the door.

They stopped in the dining room, and James took her coat and scarf off, hanging them on a chair for the time being. Gideon appeared in the archway to the living room, but James shook his head at his son before he could speak and then said, "I need you boys to start a pot of tomato soup and grilled cheese sandwiches. Mix the soup with half a can of milk and half a can of water."

Gideon groaned, and James shook his head again. "Now," he said, his voice perfectly controlled.

A half hour later, James tucked the blankets around Fern as the last light of the day faded among the tree branches outside their window. James pulled the curtains and turned the lamp to dim.

The headache was a doozy, and she'd been nauseated by the time they reached the second floor. Now she had a bucket beside the bed—but hopefully the worst of it had passed.

He would make sure the boys were getting their dinner and then come sit with her until he was certain she was down for the night.

As he descended the stairs, he heard the boys' voices, raised and raw. "You do not do everything around here," Nelson said. "I help out all the time."

"Then why didn't you flip the sandwiches?"

"Because you were standing there."

The smell of burnt bread reached James before he reached the kitchen. "I like my grilled cheese sandwiches singed," he said. "How about you guys?" James stepped into the kitchen, a forced smile on his face.

Nelson's arms were crossed, and Gideon, who had taken off his sweatshirt, balanced a sandwich on a spatula in midair.

"The top looks fine," James said.

Gideon flipped the sandwich onto a plate; the bottom was black as coal.

"I'm not going to eat that," Nelson said.

"Tough," Gideon answered. "I used the last of the cheese and the bread."

"You can have an open-face sandwich if you prefer," James said. "But no more complaining; we need to make do."

"Like Justin is having to right now?" Gideon's blue eyes flashed as he dropped the sandwich onto a plate on the counter.

"Pardon?" James rubbed the side of his head.

"Justin. Remember? His mom had a heart attack."

James sighed. As he'd put Fern to bed, he'd forgotten about Gideon's request to go to the hospital. "His dad is with him, right? He'll be able to help Justin navigate the hospital."

Gideon shook his head. "No. His dad is in Chicago—he can't get in touch with him. Their cell service got turned off." Gideon tossed the spatula in the sink, and it clattered against the stainless steel.

"Where's Justin staying tonight?"

Gideon crossed his arms. "I told him he could stay here, but he said he had other options. His grandparents live in Princeton. Maybe they're coming over."

"Then they can help him at the hospital."

Gideon shook his head. "Justin said they're really old and incompetent."

He could see his son was distressed. Plus, if Fern were in the hospital and he were out of town, he hoped someone would help his boys. "Son," James put his hand on Gideon's shoulder. "Let's figure this out, okay?" James leaned against the counter as the boys dished up their soup. He could have Nelson sit with Fern while he took Gideon to the hospital. But they should go now, in case her headache grew even worse.

"How about if we eat after we get back." He stood up straight. "Put the soup back in the pot to stay warm."

Gideon smiled.

"Nelson, I need you to go sit with Mom. Take your cell phone with you, and call me if she starts feeling worse—if anything changes."

Fifteen minutes later, James pulled into the hospital parking lot as his cell phone rang. He flipped it open to speakerphone and Nelson's frantic voice filled the van. "Mom's feeling worse."

"Hold the bucket for her," James commanded. "We're on our way home." James flipped the phone closed as he began to turn the van around.

"Dad," Gideon moaned.

James handed him the phone. "Dial the Hope Haven number and ask someone to get a message to Justin that I'll stop by tomorrow."

Gideon took the phone, dialed the number, relayed James's message, then hung up, immediately crossing his arms. They rode home in silence.

Surely Gideon can see where my priorities are. It was careless of me to leave Fern. He accelerated as he headed home.

After James sat with her, Fern's stomach settled back down. Once she fell back to sleep, James headed downstairs and collapsed onto a dining room chair as he asked Nelson how his homework was going.

"Fine," he answered. He seemed shaken by Fern's episode. "Dad," he said. "What if she'd gotten really sick?"

"You would have coped." James thought it pretty unlikely that Nelson would go into medicine someday, but one never knew. "Where's Gideon?"

Nelson shrugged. "Upstairs, I guess."

"I'm going to go back up and sit with Mom," James said to Nelson. He was afraid that another bout of nausea might overtake her. As James climbed the stairs, he had the image of

Mount Everest in his head, looming above him. It had been a long day for all of them.

The following afternoon, James stood in the hallway outside the Med/Surg Unit, chatting with Dr. Hamilton. He'd been pulled into the operating room for a few weeks because of a staffing shortage. It was easier to fill positions on the med floor than in OR.

"Good work," Dr. Hamilton said. They'd just finished a laparoscopic appendectomy.

James nodded. It was always a pleasure to work with Dr. Hamilton. James hoped he, himself, was as sharp in another decade and a half. He glanced at the clock at the end of the hall. 3:10. He would call Fern and then change.

A minute later he was in the staff lounge, fishing his cell phone out of his backpack. He had a voice mail, and he quickly punched in his security code. It was from Dr. Andrews—the MRI showed no changes.

James dialed Fern, and she picked up on the third ring. He relayed the message about the MRI quickly and then asked how she was feeling.

"Much better," she said.

He exhaled, relieved that she was on the recovery schedule from the injection that the doctor had predicted.

"Take your time with Gideon and Justin," she said. "I'm praying for the boy's mother."

"Good," James said, dismayed that he hadn't thought to pray. He exhaled again. "Thank goodness you're feeling better."

"Yes," she said. "I was thinking about starting dinner."

"Sit tight until I get home, okay?" He didn't want her in the kitchen getting dizzy or coming down with another headache or more nausea.

"Nelson will be home in a few minutes."

"Okay. But be careful." James said good-bye and changed quickly into his jeans and a sweatshirt. A few minutes later he bounded down the staircase to the second floor. As he pushed through the fire door, he caught a glimpse of Gideon at the Cardiac Care Unit desk.

"Son," he called out and approached Gideon. "Where's Justin?"

"In with his mom."

James followed Gideon down the hall. Justin looked up as they entered. He wore the same sweatshirt and jeans as earlier in the week. He nodded toward James but didn't say anything.

James stepped forward and introduced himself to Justin's mom, adding that he was Gideon's father.

"I'm Marcia Barnes." Her voice was barely audible. She was petite, about the size of Fern, and her dark hair was pulled back in a ponytail.

"How are you feeling?" James asked, moving closer to the bed.

"I'm still in a lot of pain."

He glanced at the bag attached to her IV. Surely they were giving her morphine. Next he read her monitor. Her blood pressure was high, but her pulse was steady.

"What do you think?" Justin asked. "How's she doing?"

"Cardiac actually isn't my field," James said. "But I could help with some basic questions to ask."

Justin nodded his appreciation.

"How about your dad? Is he around this afternoon?"

Justin turned his attention toward his mother. Her eyes were closed. "He's not here," Justin whispered. "Can you tell me what questions to ask?"

"Sure." James squinted, trying to think of how to phrase the questions so they would make sense to a teenager. "It would be good to know if your mom's heart problem is genetic or if it's caused from environmental problems—like diet." James opened the drawer of the bedside table and took out a pad and pen. "How about if I write down a few questions?"

Justin nodded. "That would be great. Thanks."

James wrote down the first question and then added, *Is there a cure? If so, what is it? Changes to lifestyle—diet? Exercise? What medication will be prescribed? Side effects? What other treatment options are available?*

James handed the pad to Justin and explained the questions.

Just then, Janice Thompson stepped into the room.

"Oh, hi, James," she said. Janice glanced from Marcia to Justin. "I just have a few more questions for Mrs. Barnes and for her son."

"Of course," James said. "Gideon, we need to go." James patted Justin's shoulder.

Gideon followed his father in silence until they reached the employee parking lot. "That was pointless," he said.

James felt his heart sink. "I'm not exactly sure what you were expecting me to do, Gid. The cardiac nurses are taking great care of her. And I think we gave Justin some important questions to ask."

Gideon jumped into the passenger seat. "I know you're stressed with mom and everything. But there are other needs in the world too."

James opened his door, deciding not to react. He had expected, sometime, that one of his boys would resent how much time and care their mother took, but he had thought Nelson would be the one, not Gideon. It was perfectly normal, he knew, and he and Fern both wanted to allow their sons to vent if they had to.

James climbed in as Gideon slammed his door closed. "You could at least act like you care." Gideon's voice was shrill.

"I'm trying here, Gid," James said softly. After a beat of silence, he started the van.

Chapter Seven

*A*INSLEE, OVER HERE!" ELENA STOOD AND WAVED. Ainslee made her way down the narrow aisle of the Diner on the Corner and bumped against the chalkboard with the specials listed on it. It started to totter and she grabbed it quickly, rolling her eyes as she steadied it.

Elena smiled. She had a vague memory of being big and pregnant and accidentally knocking things over.

Ainslee slipped out of her jacket as she walked. She wore a long black smock over maternity jeans. Her hair was piled on her head, and she wore huge black hoop earrings. She looked adorable.

Elena stepped out of the booth and gave her a half hug. "You look so cute."

"I feel so big." Ainslee tossed her purse and then her coat into the green vinyl booth.

"Are you hungry?" Elena asked.

"Starving." Ainslee laughed as she sat down. "But I told Doug I'd cook a big dinner tonight, so I better save room." She picked up the menu and scanned it for a minute while Elena sipped her coffee.

Lindy Yao approached to take their order. "What can I get you two?"

Elena said she would stick with coffee.

"No pie? It's lemon crème—and fresh." Lindy held her pen poised over her pad.

"It sounds delicious," Elena said. "But my calorie burner slowed down. I can't eat like I used to."

"Oh, sure," Lindy replied, her black eyes dancing. "I only hope I'm as thin as you are when I'm your age."

Elena grinned. Chances were Lindy would be thinner.

The waitress turned to Ainslee. "Coffee for you too?"

"Please, with cream. And I'll have a glass of milk too, and a half sandwich, the turkey and avocado delight. With chips please." Ainslee handed Lindy the menu with a flourish.

Elena leaned forward as the waitress left. "What are you planning to have for dinner?"

Ainslee tilted her head and put her finger to her jawline. "Let's see. Fettuccine Alfredo with shrimp, garlic bread, green salad, and chocolate cheesecake for dessert."

"You go, girl." Elena leaned back against the booth and smiled. "Speaking of dessert, I was thinking about having strawberry shortcake for the shower."

"Yum." Ainslee pulled a tube of lip balm from her purse and ran it across her lips.

"And also platters of plain fruit—for us older ladies," Elena added. "I'm sending out the invitations soon. I hope you brought your calendar."

"I didn't." Ainslee exhaled. "Can you give me a call?"

Elena nodded. "I was thinking about April twenty-fourth—but we can talk about it over the phone. Let's talk about a theme for the shower." She met Ainslee's eyes. "Do you know if it's a boy or a girl?"

Ainslee shook her head. "We want to be surprised."

Elena slid her coffee cup to the side, away from the notebook. "So pink or blue is out. Yellow might work."

"Or sage," Ainslee replied as Lindy placed a glass of milk in front of her. "That's what we've painted the nursery."

"Perfect." Elena wrote down *sage*. She swore she couldn't trust her memory past a few minutes these days. "How about a theme? I know you like antiques."

Ainslee's face brightened. "We have an old-fashioned pram that I bought. You know, one of those that an English nanny would have pushed in London during the late 1800s. It's the sweetest thing." She wiggled closer to the table. "Oh, and I found an old porcelain doll and an old fire truck too—one pulled by horses. The paint on the horses is all chipped. It's so cool. I got all of them at Once Upon A Time. Minnie gives me first choice."

"Minnie?" Elena held her pen over her pad.

"My boss. Oh, could you invite her too?"

"Sure." Elena wrote down *Minnie* and then *antique pram* and *old toys*. She glanced up at Ainslee. "How fun. This will make a great theme if you don't mind that I'm cashing in on your nursery décor."

"Not at all."

Lindy delivered the sandwich, and Ainslee popped a chip into her mouth. "You know," she said. "I'm starting to look forward to the shower."

"You weren't before?" Elena put the pen down on the notebook.

"Well, you know." Ainslee tucked a piece of turkey back into the sandwich. "You guys are mostly my mom's friends, really. And the whole mother–grandmother approach. I was feeling a little awkward. But I think it will be a lot of fun."

Elena smiled. "Get me a list of your friends and I'll invite them."

"Things have been a little tense with Mother lately," Ainslee added. "She keeps meddling. But this is good—it gives her something else to think about."

Elena suppressed a smile. It was always so fascinating to get a glimpse of another point of view. "Well, we love you and your mom. And the thing is, we want to celebrate this baby with you but also support you. Mothers—maybe more than anyone else in this world—need a good support system. It's the hardest job there is." Elena stopped.

A puzzled look passed over Ainslee's face, but she took a bite of her sandwich and relaxed.

"As far as the guest list, I have your mom, of course, Fern Bell, people from Hope Haven, your sister—"

"Hi!" Kirstie and another girl approached.

"Speaking of," Elena said.

Ainslee struggled to turn around. "Oh, hi," she said. "What are you doing here?"

"Heather and I decided to have coffee."

"Sit with us," Ainslee said, scooting over toward the wall, dragging her plate along.

"Do you mind?" Kirstie asked the other girl.

She shook her head, but she looked like she minded. Kirstie sat down next to Elena and her friend slipped in beside Ainslee.

"Elena, this is Heather Miller. Heather, Elena Rodriguez. She works with our mom."

Heather pulled her gloves off each hand. "Nice to meet you," she said but didn't extend her hand across the table.

"Likewise." Elena paused. "Loren Miller's daughter, right?" Elena knew Loren as a former board member of the hospital.

"Yep, that's me." Heather wiggled out of her wool coat. She turned to Ainslee. "When is your baby due?"

"Beginning of May." Ainslee dabbed at her mouth with her napkin.

"Late lunch?" Kirstie asked and then smiled at her sister.

"Second lunch," Ainslee answered. "Or first dinner." She grinned. "It depends on how I want to classify it."

"Will you have the baby at Hope Haven?" Heather asked.

"Where else?"

"Princeton. Peoria. I don't know. Anywhere but here . . ." Heather's voice trailed off.

The conversation turned to Kirstie's boyfriend of nearly a year, Mark Holcher, causing Kirstie to blanch. She quickly and skillfully deflected questions. Heather jumped in to discuss her current dilemma, how her delivering résumés on foot hadn't led to one interview. "Plus my parents stopped my allowance. Closed my accounts. All that stuff." Her voice was loud and dramatic. "When I think about all the money Dad gave away over the years." She chuckled but it was not a mirthful sound. "It just makes me mad."

She pushed the salt shaker back and forth. "I even applied to work at the hospital cafeteria. I mean, I'm really desperate here. But even they turned me down. Said they weren't hiring and to come back in a month."

"That's not so bad. It's better than nothing." Elena couldn't help counteracting the girl's negativity with a bit of hope.

Heather scowled. "You'd think if they're going to have an opening in a month, they could just hire me now."

Elena took a sip of coffee. She was not going to get into a power play with the young woman, that was for sure. Lindy approached just then with two more menus and the conversation shifted to food and drinks. After a minute, Elena said she needed to leave. "I'm picking Izzy up from day care today."

Ainslee thanked her profusely as Kirstie slid out of the booth to free Elena, who told all of the girls it was good to see them and then made her way through the diner, paying Lindy at the cash register.

As she left the diner she thought of the Millers and others who had been dealing with hard times. She breathed a prayer of thanks for her job and for Cesar's. They knew, from when he had been laid off, what it was like to face the woes of financial insecurity.

Chapter Eight

ANABELLE STOOD IN THE MIDDLE OF HER PANTRY trying to focus on the stocked shelves. They'd had spaghetti two nights ago, so that was out. Cameron had made chili the night before and there were leftovers. She stepped out of the pantry. She wouldn't have to make dinner after all. She inhaled deeply. Except they'd both had the leftover chili for lunch—she couldn't expect Cameron to eat the same thing three meals in a row. She stepped back into the pantry as she heard the back door open and then close.

"What's for dinner?" Cameron asked, his voice full and cheery.

"I don't know." Anabelle's voice fell flat.

Cameron stopped behind her and wrapped his arms around her shoulders, nuzzling the back of her neck. "How about dinner in town?"

They hadn't been out for a couple of weeks. "Anything to save me from the dreaded dinner decision." She patted his arm,

79

and he let go of her, stepping aside for her to slip out of the pantry first. "I'm going to change though." She'd been working in the yard, raking last fall's dead leaves out of the flowerbeds.

As she hurried up the stairs the phone rang. Maybe it was Ainslee. She hurried back to the kitchen but Cameron had already answered.

"Who is it?" she asked.

He hung up. "Wrong number."

"Oh." As she ascended the stairs again, she wondered when Ainslee would call. It had been days since she'd heard from her. Yesterday hadn't been bad—she'd been so busy at work that she hadn't had time to think about Ainslee and the baby much, and today she had tried her best to keep her mind off the topic.

Things were so different now. When she was a young woman she didn't talk to her mother every day. Kirstie had called last evening and then again after school today. She called nearly every day. And Ainslee usually did. Evan was a different story— she made sure to call him a few times a week. He kept in contact with Cameron because of the business, calling with questions about services and billings, but he seldom called Anabelle to chat.

She pulled a pair of slacks and a blouse from her closet and fished her fashion boots from the corner.

It wouldn't hurt to call Ainslee. She sat down on the edge of the bed, picked up the cordless phone, and quickly punched in the numbers. Doug answered after five rings.

"Hi." Anabelle was afraid that her voice was overly cheery. "I was just calling to see how all of you are doing."

"Good," Doug said. "I just walked in the door though—let me find Ainslee." The muffled sound of Doug calling out came through the receiver and a few moments later he came back on the line. "She's taking a shower," Doug said. "Can she call you back?"

"Sure," Anabelle said. "Is she feeling all right?"

"Yeah, I think so," Doug said. "She's been sleeping the last couple of nights, so that's good."

Anabelle smiled and wanted to say, "Just wait" but didn't. Instead she said, "Cameron and I are going out this evening, but we should be home by eight."

"I'll tell her."

Impulsively she said, "We're going to the Parlor for dinner. Want to join us?"

Doug paused for a minute, and Anabelle wondered if Ainslee was really in the shower or if she was feeding him lines. Finally Doug said, sounding a little uncomfortable, "Thanks but I think we need a stay-at-home evening."

Anabelle half hoped that he would invite them to stop by after dinner, and she almost offered to stop by the market and buy ice cream to bring, but he didn't say anymore and she bit her tongue.

"Talk to you later," he said.

"Okay. Bye." Anabelle sat with the receiver in her hand for a moment. It was ridiculous for her to be walking on eggshells around her own daughter.

"Ready?" Cameron called up the stairs.

"Be down in a minute," Anabelle answered, slipping her sweatshirt off over her head.

Anabelle closed the menu and slipped her reading glasses from her nose, letting them hang around her neck. "Maybe you could take her out to lunch," she said to Cameron.

He looked at her over the edge of the menu, his blue eyes twinkling. "Annie, I'm not opposed to asking Ainslee out to lunch, but I am opposed to being a mole."

"I am not asking you to be a mole." Anabelle laced her fingers around the string of beads that held her glasses.

Cameron put his menu down. "You want me to get involved in a situation between you and our daughter. What would you call that?"

"Diplomacy." Anabelle smiled.

"My point exactly." Cameron raised the menu again. "Do you work tomorrow?"

"Yes." She was hoping Cameron would take Ainslee out while she was at the hospital. It would seem less suspicious that way.

Kerri Lane, their favorite waitress at the restaurant, stopped at their table. "How are my two favorite customers?" She wore a red-bibbed apron over a white blouse and black slacks, and her blonde hair was pulled back in a high ponytail.

"We're good," Anabelle answered as Kerri began pouring her a cup of decaf.

"Ready to be grandparents?" Kerri had graduated high school with Ainslee.

"You bet." Cameron put his menu down. "How old is your little one now?"

"Almost two." Kerri placed the coffee pot on the table and took her pad and pen from her pocket. "And boy is she busy.

Just stayed the night with my parents for the first time last week. They had a blast." They chatted for another minute and then Kerri took their order: apricot chicken from the heart-healthy menu for both of them.

As Kerri walked away, Anabelle wondered if Ainslee would let her baby stay with them by the time she was two. It was hard to imagine now.

Cameron had a puzzled look on his face. "What were we talking about?"

"Ainslee."

"I thought we were done with that topic."

Anabelle shook her head as his cell phone rang.

"Oops," he pulled it from the case on his belt. "I forgot to turn it off." He turned the ringer down as he looked at the screen. "It's Ainslee." He looked at Anabelle.

"Answer it," she said.

"Hello, sweetheart." Cameron kept his voice low and glanced around to see if he was disturbing anyone. "Lunch tomorrow?" He smiled at Anabelle. "Sure. At the Parlor?"

There was a pause and then he said, "I'll meet you here—I mean there. Bye."

He chuckled as he turned off his phone and put it away. "Like mother like daughter," he said, a twinkle in his eye.

"Unbelievable," Anabelle said, wondering what Ainslee was up to.

The next morning the Cardiac Care Unit's population was down a little—three beds were vacant. Anabelle hoped she wouldn't be running her entire shift like earlier in the week. After report, she entered Marcia's room. Debbie, the night-shift nurse, stood at the computer, finishing up her charting. "She's had a restless night," she said, "but she's sleeping soundly now."

Anabelle nodded. "Is her husband back?" She straightened the extra blanket that had half slid off the bed.

"Haven't seen him," Debbie said. "And Marcia didn't mention him. There are some notes from the social worker."

"Good."

They chatted for a few minutes about medications and procedures. Dr. Hildebrand would make her rounds by midmorning, which would also shed more light on Marcia's case. Her angiogram showed a blockage, but Anabelle hadn't heard if she would have surgery or a balloon angioplasty.

"She's still really weak," Debbie said. "And having residual pain. The doctor ordered a stress test but wants to wait a few days before it's administered."

Marcia stirred a little in her sleep. Her dark hair was fanned over the pillow, and she looked much younger than forty-four, more like thirty-four.

"She says there's no history of heart disease in her family," Debbie said, "but you have to wonder. Don't you think? How often does a woman her age have a major coronary?"

Anabelle nodded. She remembered from Marcia's family history that her maternal grandmother had died in her early forties. Maybe it had been a misdiagnosed heart attack.

"She's worried about how she's going to pay her bills too," Debbie said. "She's not sure if her husband's insurance is still active."

"Oh dear," Anabelle said. "What does the business office say about that?"

"They're looking into it."

After Debbie left, Anabelle logged into the computer. Janice had added notes about the bruises and had also added that Justin was uncooperative in discussing his mother's injuries. Marcia stirred again. Poor woman. An absent husband, possible unpaid insurance, and a surly son just added insult to injury.

"How did it go?" Anabelle asked Cameron as she clutched the receiver of the phone to her ear. Barbara had gone down to the cafeteria for a late lunch.

"Good."

"Are you home?"

"Yep. Just pulled up." And he actually had his cell with him.

Anabelle swirled the chair away from the desk. "What's up?" She hated his terse responses.

"Not much. Ainslee's feeling fine now and looking forward to the baby coming." Cameron paused. "And you know, I'm really getting excited about being a grandfather."

"Cameron." Anabelle stood.

"What?"

"What did she say about me? About the morning in the ER?"

Cameron didn't answer for a moment and then said, slowly, "Nothing."

"Why did she want to have lunch with you then?"

"Anabelle." She heard a car door slam. "I think she wanted to see me. I am her dad, remember?"

Anabelle laced her fingers through the beaded chain around her neck. She couldn't believe that Ainslee didn't have something up her sleeve in asking Cameron to lunch. "Did she say anything about the birth? About not wanting me there?"

"No." She heard Sarge barking in the background. "We talked about her job. About Doug's paternity leave. About my projects. It was a normal conversation."

"Oh." Anabelle wheeled back toward the desk.

"Sorry to disappoint you," he said.

"You didn't bring any of that other stuff up?"

"No."

She hated his one-word answers. "Okay, then. I'll see you after work."

"Love you," he said, his voice trailing off. She imagined him pulling the mail out of the box and thumbing through it as he said good-bye.

She hung up the phone and stared at the computer monitor. Cameron never took problems with the kids as seriously as she did. On one hand she envied him, but on the other hand she resented it because it meant it was up to her to sort most of the problems out. He could be the fun parent. The happy-go-lucky one discussing jobs and projects.

"Anabelle."

Her head jerked up to find Janice standing in front of her. "How is Marcia doing?"

"About the same. Her pain level is pretty high and she's still exhausted."

"Has she given you any more info on her bruises?"

Anabelle shook her head.

"I contacted Family Services. There aren't any previous reports on her husband or her son." Janice held a file against her chest. "I went ahead and reported the bruises, but until I can interview her husband, there isn't much else to do." Just as Janice finished speaking, her pager went off. She pressed the button on the side of it and then said, "Off to the ER." She gave Anabelle a half wave. "Keep me posted on Marcia." Before Anabelle could answer, the social worker had pushed through the door to the staircase.

Anabelle had seen plenty of secrets come out in the hospital. Who could know what was really going on with the Barnes family? Or with any family, for that matter, even her own.

Cameron's lunch with Ainslee inspired Anabelle to take a chance, so, as she hurried toward her car after her shift ended, she hit speed dial number four for Ainslee. Just then Eddie Blaine came toward her, pushing a wheelbarrow full of twigs.

"It looks like the vandal is behaving," she said cheerfully as the phone rang.

"So far so good," Eddie said. "We've been vandalism free for two whole days." He gave her a thumbs-up as Ainslee answered her phone.

Anabelle smiled at Eddie and then said, "Hi, sweetie. How are you?"

"Just fine."

Anabelle concentrated on keeping her tone even. "Dad said the two of you had a good lunch."

LESLIE GOULD • 88

"It was fun," Ainslee answered. "He and I should do that more often."

"How are you feeling?"

"Great."

"And how's the baby?"

"Just fine, Mother."

"Are you tired?" Anabelle said, reaching her car.

"A little. In fact I was reading and dozing."

"Oh, don't let me keep you," Anabelle said, climbing into the driver's seat. "I'll call later."

"Okay. Talk to you then." Ainslee's "good-bye" trailed off and the line went dead.

Anabelle hit End and leaned back against the headrest. She hated tension with her children. She wanted to fix it or unravel it or discover exactly what was wrong and then sort it out. She frowned. But honestly, she'd never been able to do that, not since they left infancy. But this time she had to. Her relationship with her grandchild was at stake.

Chapter Nine

ANDACE STEPPED THROUGH THE SLIDING GLASS doors of Hope Haven into the chilly afternoon. It was three thirty. Howie had been home for nearly an hour and Brooke would be on her way soon. She fished her phone out of her pocket and noted she had one voice mail. She listened as she headed toward her car. Heath Carlson honked as he passed her and waved. Candace smiled and waved back.

"This is Dr. Lloyd's office. We've had a cancellation for this afternoon at five. Call me back if you would like to bring Howie in then."

If she wanted to make it in time, she would need to pick Howie up immediately. She climbed into her car, clicked the missed calls list on her cell phone, found the number, and hit Send. If the appointment was still open, it would be worth the trip to Peoria this afternoon instead of waiting another three weeks.

The receptionist answered, confirmed the slot was still available, and booked the appointment. Next, Candace called her mother and asked her to have him ready even though he wasn't going to want to go. She knew he wouldn't be happy about having an appointment sprung on him like this.

Janet said she would pry him away from the TV and have him ready. Candace thanked her and hit End.

As she pulled up to the house, Janet and Howie came out the door. He wore his red jacket, unzipped, and held his stocking cap in his hand. Her mother had a grip on his arm and a frown on her face.

"Thank you," Candace said, hopping out of her seat and opening the back door. She scooped Howie into her arms and deposited him on his booster seat before he could protest, clicking the restraint into position.

"You're right," Janet said. "He doesn't want to go. Good luck."

Candace tried to smile. "We should be back by seven thirty or so."

"I'll keep dinner warm." Janet pulled her sweater tighter. Candace felt for her mother, who'd taken on a parenting role with her grandchildren; she knew it wasn't always easy.

"Bye." She jumped back in the car and backed out of the driveway.

"I'm hungry," Howie said.

"Did you have a snack after school?"

"Nope," he answered.

Candace couldn't imagine that. Her mother was a firm believer in afternoon snacks. "Did Grammy offer you some apples? Maybe some peanut butter? Or crackers and cheese?"

Howie slapped the restraint of his seat. "I wanted cookies."

"So, Grammy did offer you a snack? But you refused it."

He didn't answer.

"Howie, I wouldn't let you have cookies either until you had healthy food. And," she paused for effect, "you need to be accurate. You need to give me all the information from the start—not just the information that helps your cause."

"I'm hungry," he said again.

Candace stopped for a red light on Fifth Avenue and dug a granola bar out of her purse, handing it back through the seats.

"These are yucky," Howie said.

"That's what we have. Eat it or don't. But don't complain anymore." She wished she'd had time to change into something more professional than a long-sleeved T-shirt, jeans, and a fleece. At least she had worn her boots today and not running shoes. She sighed, wishing she didn't care what other people thought of her. But it wasn't just that. She felt more confident when she was dressed up a little, more like a professional mom. She nearly laughed at herself. She wondered if any mother ever felt like a professional mom. She turned on the radio. Anabelle might. And Elena. For that matter her mother probably did, and her sister Susan certainly acted like she had it all down.

She accelerated onto the highway and headed toward Peoria. A tractor pulled a seeder over a plowed field and a flock of starlings swooped over the freshly turned soil in the distance. The light of the day was waning and a sense of melancholy came over Candace. She glanced in her rearview mirror. Howie was fast asleep, the unopened granola bar in his fist.

Almost an hour and a half later, she pulled into the parking lot of the office building on the outskirts of Peoria. "Sweetie," Candace said, lifting Howie from his seat. He wrapped his arms around her neck and his legs around her middle. "Can you walk?" she asked, closing his door with her hip.

He shook his head, jarring her chin.

She waddled toward the front of the building. She had less than a minute until the appointment started. Maybe it had been a mistake to take one so late in the day when Howie would be out of sorts—she should have guessed he would fall asleep in the car.

She pushed through the glass door and then poked at the elevator button with her finger, jabbing at it twice before connecting. She shifted Howie to the side as she shuffled into the elevator. "I need you to push the 3 button," she said.

He shook his head again and then buried it on her shoulder. She pushed the button as a wave of anxiety swept through her. She'd intended to do more research on ADD before the doctor's appointment, to educate herself and come up with a list of questions. They reached the third floor, and Candace waddled off the elevator, spotted Dr. Lloyd's name on the wall, and made her way into his office.

"This must be Howie," the receptionist said.

Candace nodded.

The receptionist pulled a stack of papers from a file. "I need you to fill these out. The doctor is running a little late so you should have time."

Candace took the papers and tried to slide Howie onto a chair, but he began to cry. "Sweetie," she said. "I'm going to sit right here beside you."

"I want you," he said.

She pulled him onto her lap, looking over his shoulder at the paperwork. She needed her insurance card and employment information. She put the papers down on the chair next to her and began digging in her purse. She was hungry too—and tired.

At five thirty the doctor called them into his office. Howie still clung to her, and she stumbled a little in the waiting room as she stood, but the doctor didn't seem to notice. He led the way, his perfectly pressed lab coat a beacon of brightness in the subtly lit hallway. He looked young, around thirty, and wore expensive shoes. His hair was thick with mousse or gel, some sort of product, and his fingernails looked like they were professionally manicured.

He stepped back and motioned for Candace to lead the way into the room as he glanced at the paperwork. Candace collapsed into the first chair she came to.

"How about if you take the guest of honor place," the doctor said to Howie, pointing to the examination table.

Howie shook his head and whispered to Candace, "I don't want a shot."

"You're not getting a shot," she said to him in a normal tone. At least she hoped he wasn't.

"No shots," Dr. Lloyd boomed. "We're going to talk for a few minutes, that's all."

Howie clung to Candace.

"He slept in the car," she said, feeling as if she were making an excuse for him, but Dr. Lloyd didn't seem to be listening. His head was buried in the paperwork. "I see his teacher is the one who recommended he see me. They usually know first," he said.

Howie shifted his weight, and Candace turned him around on her lap and took off his coat.

"So you don't feel his behavior is a problem at home?" the doctor asked.

"It seems like normal little boy behavior," Candace answered.

"Do you have other sons?" he asked.

Candace shook her head.

The doctor slipped the paperwork back into the file and put it on the counter behind him. "I like to think of all of us as cars, vans, or busses," he said. Howie lifted his head and Dr. Lloyd continued. "Some of us are like a school bus—it takes a long time for us to get where we're going but we take a lot of ideas with us. Others are like vans—the trip is a little faster, but still we can take a full load. And then others are like a sports car who zip along and arrive in no time."

Howie turned his head back to Candace and smiled.

"Howie, what do you think you are?"

"A sports car," he answered with his most animated expression all day. "Or maybe a Star Wars X-Wing."

Dr. Lloyd clapped his hands together, obviously pleased. "Well, well, there's no doubt that you're bright."

Candace felt her frustration growing, not sure how a talk about busses, vans, and sports cars—or how bright he was based on one comment—could help diagnose Howie's problem, if he had a problem.

"I like to go fast," Howie said.

"Except when it's time to go out the door for school or climb into bed," Candace wanted to add but didn't.

"There are several different theories," Dr. Lloyd continued. "That during the hunter-gatherer period, ADD enabled hunters to do needed jobs to provide for their families. Of course today those traits aren't necessary."

"Except for race-car drivers," Candace said. "What about other theories?"

"Oh, the usual suspects. Environmental, neurological, that sort of thing. Did you take any medication during his pregnancy?"

Candace shook her head. "How exactly do you come up with a diagnosis?"

"We have the parent interview—which we're doing now. Next, I'll ask Howie some questions. I'll want you to observe him closely at home." Dr. Lloyd glanced back down at the paperwork. "We also rule other things out."

"Like?"

"Have there been any changes at school?"

"He has a new teacher."

Dr. Lloyd made a note. "How about at home?"

Candace shook her head.

The doctor asked several more questions and kept taking notes. After a few minutes Howie slipped off her lap and began playing with the blocks in a corner, stacking them into a tower.

"I see that his father is deceased," Dr. Lloyd said. He looked Candace in the eye and said, "I'm sorry."

"Thank you," she whispered. The man's kindness touched her.

He gripped his pen. "There are several possibilities here," he said. "Howie could have ADD or ADHD—ADHD has the added hyperactivity factor—and medication could be the solution. Or he could be unsettled by having a new teacher. Or perhaps he's entering into a new stage of grief concerning his father."

He took out a pad from his pocket. "I'm going to write a prescription and leave it up to you whether to fill it or not." He smiled. "Most parents like to take a prescription home with them; it makes them feel better."

Candace grimaced.

"Take some time and observe Howie. Get him to talk about his feelings about the new teacher and about his dad. See how he reacts." He signed his name with a flourish. "At any time, start him on the medication if you feel it's what's best. Either way, make an appointment in a month to check back in."

Candace took the prescription from the doctor as Howie mowed over a stack of blocks. The doctor pulled his chair closer and tried to get Howie's attention. Howie nodded at him but that was all.

"How do you like school?" the doctor asked.

"Fine." Howie stacked the blocks rapidly.

"Do you like your teacher?"

Howie shrugged. "I liked my first one better."

"How about at home—what's your favorite thing to do?"

"Watch TV," Howie said.

Candace blanched, wishing he had said playing with Legos.

"You can try cutting the TV time," the doctor whispered to her and then practically winked. Candace was sure he didn't have kids of his own.

Dr. Lloyd stood. "I'll ask him more questions at our next appointment. That's enough for today." He reached down toward Howie. "It's been nice to meet you, young man."

Howie took his hand briefly but then turned back to the blocks.

"We need to put the toys away and go home," Candace said. "Brooke and Grammy are waiting for us."

The doctor shook Candace's hand quickly and slipped through the doorway.

"I want to keep playing," Howie wailed.

Candace kneeled down on the floor. "I'll help you."

Howie pouted as Candace put most of the blocks away and then stated, adamantly, that he was still hungry. He put up his arms to be held.

"How about if we stop by McDonalds?" Candace handed Howie his coat. "But you need to walk to the car. You're getting too heavy for Mommy to carry you all the time. Is it a deal?"

"It's a deal." He put up his hand for a high five and then slapped Candace's palm with all of his might. A moment later they were at the receptionist's desk, making the next appointment.

Dr. Lloyd stood behind the receptionist, watching Howie as Candace paid the co-pay.

"We're going to McDonalds," Howie called out to the doctor.

The receptionist smiled and Dr. Lloyd began to laugh.

Candace's face reddened as she put her wallet back in her purse. It certainly didn't take much to make her feel like a bad mom.

Chapter Ten

YOU'RE GOING BACK TO THE HOSPITAL?" CAMERON asked as Anabelle grabbed her coat the following Wednesday evening.

"They're short in the ER and they just got a call that a cardiac patient is coming in." She slipped her arms into the sleeves of her coat.

"Do you think you're overdoing it?"

"It's just for a few hours," she answered, slinging her purse over her shoulder.

"Don't overdo it." Cameron kissed her on the lips. "Or you'll really make me feel guilty in my retirement."

Anabelle laughed. She didn't envy Cameron his retirement—not yet anyway. Maybe she would after the baby was born.

On the way into town, she tried to remember the last time she'd helped out in ER. It had been after the big storm last fall. She enjoyed the excitement, especially when it was busy, and helping out with a cardiac patient was right up her alley. She knew Cameron had a glimpse of how fulfilling her job was for her, but he couldn't understand the thrill of helping with a trauma patient or being able to do exactly the right thing to save a life or even improve a life.

Thirty minutes later, wearing a fresh pair of scrubs, Anabelle reported for duty in the ER. The sound of a siren wailed closer, and she stepped forward as the automatic doors opened with a sucking sound and into the cold night. The ambulance stopped, and an EMT swung open the passenger door and jumped down to the asphalt. A sleek silver car that seemed as if it had been following the ambulance swung into an ER parking space and both doors flung open. Two women climbed out.

Anabelle squinted into the night. She recognized both of them: Leanne and Heather Miller. She turned back toward the ambulance as an EMT jumped from the back and began pulling out the gurney. The patient's white dress shirt was yanked open, and his undershirt was pulled up around his neck. The man had gray hair and an ashen face that was mostly covered by an oxygen mask.

It was Loren Miller, a past member of Hope Haven's board and one of the most philanthropic people in Deerford. Kirstie had gone through her entire school career with Heather, and Anabelle and Cameron used to sit with Loren and Leanne at sporting events and school plays. Loren was a kind, gentle man who would do anything he possibly could for Deerford, and Hope Haven in particular. Through the years, after Kirstie and Heather had graduated, she hadn't seen the couple much, just bumping into Leanne occasionally at the grocery store. Kirstie had mentioned that Heather was back in town and that they'd had coffee recently.

Anabelle stepped back through the sliding door and waved to the secretary. "Get the doc," she said. "Tell him we need him in room 5."

The EMTs, Loren, his wife and daughter all pushed through the doors in a solid mass. The women's coats were unbuttoned and neither had a purse with her.

"Leanne," Anabelle said. "And Heather. We need you to stay here so we can care for Loren." She pointed to the waiting area. "We'll come get you as soon as we can."

Leanne clung to Loren's hand but she let go and stopped. Heather, who was Kirstie's age, kept walking.

"Heather," Anabelle stepped in front of the young woman. "Your mom needs you with her."

For a moment, Anabelle thought Heather might challenge her, but then the young woman followed her mother to the waiting room, her high-heeled boots clicking loudly over the linoleum.

Anabelle led the way to suite 5 and the EMTs transferred Loren onto the ER gurney as Anabelle washed her hands, snapped on gloves, and quickly slipped the IV bag the EMTs had started onto the pole. "I'm going to ask you a few questions," she said, her voice low.

Loren nodded.

"When did your chest pains begin?" She stuck electrode pads onto his chest as she spoke, one after the other.

"An hour ago," he answered, his words a little muffled through the mask.

"How bad is the pain, on a scale of one to ten, ten being the worst?" She reached across him to affix the far pad to his side and then looked up at the monitor.

"Pretty bad," he said in his matter-of-fact voice. "It feels like an elephant landed on my chest—and stayed." He paused. "Probably a ten," Loren said.

Anabelle opened the top drawer of the med cabinet and pulled out a four-milligram syringe of morphine. She injected it into the IV line as the EKG beeped and printed out the reading; Anabelle immediately pulled it off the machine. The blips were spiked. The EKG was completely normal. "Is the doc available?" she called out to the secretary.

"Now I am." Doctor Weller made his way across the hall, peeling off his gloves as he walked. A goofy grin spread across his freckled face as he entered the suite. "Hello," he said to Loren, as if they were meeting to play golf. The doc dropped his gloves in the trash and began scrubbing. "How long have you had chest pains?" If he recognized Loren he didn't act like it.

"An hour," Loren whispered.

An hour later, the doc met with Leanne and Heather in the waiting room and then they came back to see Loren.

Heather stood by the curtain, a scowl on her face. "I think we should have him moved to Chicago. Or at the least Peoria."

Loren shook his head. "I'm fine here."

"There's no sign of cardiac arrest," Anabelle said. "The blood work came back normal."

"The doctor said it seems to be a panic attack," Leanne said, brushing away a strand of blonde hair that fell over her face.

Loren closed his eyes. He'd been given a sedative and needed to sleep before he went home. "Has he been under extra stress?" Anabelle asked quietly.

Heather groaned. "I'll say."

"Sweetie," Leanne said to her daughter, "could you go get me a cup of coffee?"

Heather flipped her blonde hair over her shoulder and clutched her coat more tightly. "Down in the cafeteria?"

Leanne nodded. "Please."

Heather turned on her heels and marched down the hall.

Leanne glanced at Loren who had his eyes closed and was breathing calmly. "We have been under a lot of stress," she said. "Loren especially."

Anabelle knew that Loren worked in business real estate; and she could imagine, with the downturn in the economy, how things had changed for them in the last couple of years.

"We've lost investments, property, and deals that haven't gone through because builders can't get loans," Leanne said. "And Heather came home from culinary school. She's been trying to find a job—she even applied here in the cafeteria, but they're not hiring either."

Anabelle stepped closer to Leanne and put her hand on her arm. "I'm so sorry."

Leanne smiled. "It's hardest on Loren. He's always been able to provide and now he feels responsible—as if he should be able to fix everything. I keep telling him that it doesn't matter if we lose everything—things will work out." She lowered her voice even more. "Actually, having Heather home has made things more stressful. She's very put out."

Anabelle nodded in sympathy. Heather had always had a critical streak; she could imagine how having Heather around would make Loren feel even worse.

"I shouldn't burden you with our problems," Leanne said.

"You're not burdening me." Anabelle gently squeezed the woman's arm. "Would Loren talk with anyone? A pastor? A counselor? The hospital chaplain?"

"Maybe if someone recommended it besides me." Leanne turned toward her husband.

"I'll write down a few names and numbers," Anabelle said. "You sit with Loren. I'll be back in a few minutes."

After handing the list to Leanne, Anabelle glanced at her watch. It was almost ten. She called Cameron to say she would be later than she expected and of course he wasn't surprised, so she decided to peek in on Marcia while she was there.

"How are you doing?" Anabelle asked.

"Not so well. Justin was here this evening—he just left."

"This late?"

Marcia nodded. "I thought he was staying with a friend of his, but now I'm not so sure."

"Where do you think he's staying?"

Marcia winced. "Oh, I don't know. He can be so hard to figure out."

"And how about your husband? Is he back from Chicago?"

A dark cloud passed over Marcia's face and she shook her head, just slightly.

"Is Janice helping you find him?"

Marcia nodded. "She had a few ideas."

Anabelle told the woman good night and that she would see her bright and early in the morning and then headed up to the third floor to change her clothes, tempted to spend the night. She'd done that a few times when she was in her twenties, before the children were born. There were sleeping rooms for the staff on the third floor, but she was too old for that now. She'd rather have fewer hours in her own bed.

She yawned as she left the building. She used to work double shifts, too, way back when, even when the kids were in high school. She didn't know how she did it.

As she stepped from the curb to the parking lot, she heard a crash and shattering glass. "Oh dear," she said, stepping back as an alarm began to sound. She hurried down the sidewalk along the outside of the cafeteria. As she turned the corner she gasped. The stained glass of the chapel had been vandalized: jagged sapphire, crimson, and emerald glass surrounded a hole in the window; the display light, pointed at what was now a gaping hole, illuminated shards of glass along the sidewalk and grass.

She stepped out into the parking lot. Ahead, down the middle of Bureau Street, a figure ran in the shadows of the trees.

Tears sprang to Anabelle's eyes at the thought of the beautiful stained-glass window as Hap Winston came bursting through the emergency exit, his fringe of white hair wild around his head. "Did you see anyone?" he shouted.

"Maybe—down Bureau Street." There was no way to know whether the figure was the vandal or not.

Hap took off, his thin frame wobbling a little from side to side, and Anabelle followed the custodian who had to be near seventy and shouldn't be running anywhere. "Hap!" she called out. "Did you call 911?"

He stopped.

"I'll do it," she said, fishing her cell phone out of the pocket of her coat. Her voice shook as she reported the crime. Why would anyone destroy something so beautiful? The vandal had gone too far. He'd just gouged the heart of Hope Haven.

Chapter Eleven

THE SUNRISE STREAKED THE EASTERN SKY WITH PINKS and purples Thursday morning as James drove his van toward the staff parking lot of Hope Haven. He pulled around the corner and slowed in alarm. A patrol car was parked along the curb, the outside gate to the courtyard stood open, and yellow crime tape encircled the wooden fence.

A minute later James parked his van in employee parking and then hurried back to the courtyard. Plywood covered the chapel's stained-glass window. James's stomach sank. An officer stood with his back to James, but he was sure it was Elena's husband.

"Cesar," James called out. "What happened?"

"Someone threw a brick through the window." Cesar was the same height as James and stockier, and he projected a strong presence in his dark blue uniform. "An officer came out last night when it happened, but I wanted to see if I could come up with any new leads in the daylight. I've been assigned to the case."

"Did you find anything?" James asked.

Cesar shook his head. "No—just more glass." The radio strapped to his shoulder began to cackle.

"How horrible." James sighed then held up his hand in a wave. "I'll catch you later." He pulled himself away from the crime scene.

He hurried down the sidewalk trying to calm his anger as he checked his watch—he was still running early—and decided to stop by the chapel and see what the damage looked like from the inside. The doors to the room were open and James stepped inside. Usually the room, if there was even a hint of daylight, was bathed in jewel tones, but this morning it looked like a dark cave. James stood still for a moment as his eyes adjusted. Pastor Tom sat in the first pew.

As James moved down the aisle, the chaplain turned toward him, looking lost for a moment, but then he smiled and held out his hand to James. "I've been sitting here praying for whoever did this. They must have a horribly heavy heart."

As the two men shook hands, James was humbled by Pastor Tom's presence of faith to pray for the perpetrator in contrast to his own anger. "Do they have any leads?" James asked.

"No. The police report from last night says that Anabelle saw someone running on Bureau Street, but it was too dark for her to get a description."

"What time was that?"

"Ten or so."

James wondered why Anabelle would have been at the hospital that late but didn't ask. "Well, I hope the police catch the vandal soon."

"So do I," Pastor Tom said. "He needs help."

James agreed and then said good-bye. He was overcome with an uneasy feeling. As he left the chapel, he realized it was a feeling of dread, the same way he felt when Fern had been diagnosed with MS and the way he felt when he had been in Saudi Arabia and scud missiles were raining down on the tent hospital where he worked.

As James and the OR team finished the third surgery of the day, the topic of conversation switched to the stained-glass window. "There's a bucket in the cafeteria to raise money to replace it—turns out it's not covered under the insurance policy," Dr. Hamilton said as James counted the last of the sponges and charted the number on the computer.

James shook his head. "What a shame."

"A reporter from the *Deerford Dispatch* was out this morning asking questions," Dr. Hamilton added.

James pulled the suction line out of the way as the doctor tied the last suture. "Good," James said, his breath forceful against his mask. "The more attention this gets, the more likely the vandal will be caught." Plus, maybe community members would donate toward the window too.

The doctor nodded, his white mask and blue hat bobbing up and down. "Unbelievable. In my thirty years at Hope Haven, nothing like this has happened."

James turned his attention back to the seventy-three-year-old patient. They had gone through two ribs on the left side of his chest, cutting a hole in the blocked artery and tying a vein over it. "That's it," Dr. Hamilton said. He placed the needle clamp on the stand and then applied the dressing.

The patient would recover quickly and be home in two or three days, in much less time than if they had to do open-heart surgery. James stepped in front of the computer cart and charted the end time: 2:55 PM. They were right on schedule.

"How is Fern doing?" Dr. Hamilton asked as he moved away from the table.

"She started on a new medication," James said. "An injection."

"That's no fun." Dr. Hamilton slipped out of his outer gown and removed his gloves.

James nodded as he pulled the blankets up to the patient's chin.

"She's lucky to have you around. Not everyone has a personal nurse."

James smiled. He wasn't looking forward to giving Fern her injections, and he wasn't sure why, except that it was another thing that would hurt her. She already had so much pain to deal with on a daily basis as it was.

"And how about those boys of yours?" Dr. Hamilton stepped toward the computer. "Are they giving you a run for your money?"

"Maybe a jog." James met the doctor's eyes and they both smiled.

"Just wait." The doctor's laugh lines danced under his blue cap. "Sooner or later they'll have you racing." He concentrated for a minute, most likely finishing up the last of his charting and then said, "I'm off to do my rounds, but I'll stop by recovery in a little bit."

James readied the patient for the short trip down the hall. Hopefully Dr. Hamilton's caution about the boys wasn't prophetic. James was beginning to worry about Gideon's friendship with Justin though, and he and Fern had talked at length about it last night. They concluded they were both concerned with the amount of energy Gideon seemed to be investing into the friendship, and they wondered what sort of an influence Justin was or might be in the future.

Half an hour later, James tucked his cell phone into the pocket of his jacket as he headed down the hall of the Cardiac Care Unit. He stopped at the CCU nurses' station and said hello to Barbara.

"Is Anabelle around?"

Barbara pointed down the hall. "She's probably in suite 3."

A moment later James nearly collided with Anabelle as she came barreling out of the room. "James," she said with a laugh. "You're lucky to be done already."

"One of the benefits of working OR. How are you?" he asked.

"Tired. I came in last night to help in the ER—"

"And nearly caught a vandal, I heard."

"Hardly, although I wish. He was running down the street like a bat out of—well, you know where." Her eyes twinkled. "There was no way I could have caught him."

"Any ideas who it was?"

"None." Anabelle shook her head. "Are you stopping by to see Marcia?"

James nodded. "How is she?"

Anabelle lowered her voice. "Not very well. She's still weak and sleeps most of the time." The poor woman had gone through complication after complication, keeping her in the hospital an entire week. And her husband still hadn't returned from Chicago. Anabelle glanced down the hall and then stepped closer to the wall. "Justin stopped by last night to see his mom. He was upset."

"Oh." James ran his fingers through his hair. "Was he on the grounds at the same time the window was broken?" His voice was barely audible.

Anabelle put her hands up. "That's not what I was implying. Honestly."

James inhaled, trying to dispel his feeling of dread.

"I don't think we have any reason to be suspicious," Anabelle said. "I just wanted you to know that he was having a hard time—that he seems to be out of sorts. And," Anabelle paused for a second. "I hope I'm not meddling, but I wondered if you know what family in town he's staying with."

"Family? I thought his grandparents came to stay with him."

"He told me—or maybe Marcia did—that he was staying with someone in town." Anabelle touched her chin with her index finger.

James shook his head. "Something's up." James took the few steps to Marcia's door and knocked softly.

"Justin?" came her reply.

"No." He stepped into the doorway. "It's James. Gideon's father."

Her dark hair was pulled back from her pale face, and her collarbones jutted out above the collar of her hospital gown. "I remember," she said.

"Gideon and Justin are on their way, but I wanted to touch base with you before they arrived."

"Is everything okay?" Marcia asked. She scooted up a little on the bed and then winced. "Is it too much to have Justin staying with you?"

"That's just it," James said. "He's not staying with us. He told Gideon his grandparents were in town."

"Then he's staying by himself." Marcia's eyes filled with tears. "And the electricity is off. We didn't pay the bill."

James noted she said *didn't*, but he was sure she meant *couldn't*. "Have you heard from your husband?" he asked.

"No." A tear slid down her face. "That social worker has been making some phone calls, trying to track him down."

"Janice is just doing her job." James stepped closer to the bed.

"Oh, I know," Marcia said. "Don't get me wrong—I want Dan home, too, but I'm not so sure why she wants him back in Deerford so badly."

James decided that there was more going on than he knew and at the moment, it wasn't any of his business. "Justin can stay with us if he needs to."

She took a deep breath. "I'll tell him to call my parents. They'll—" Before she could finish her sentence, Justin entered the room followed by Gideon.

"Mom." Justin's voice was full of concern. "What's wrong?"

"You told me you were staying with Gideon's family."

Justin's face reddened. "I can explain."

"No. Call your grandparents."

"How can I call Grandma? My phone isn't working and neither is yours."

Gideon stepped forward with his cell extended to Justin who started to take the phone but then jerked his hand back. "I can't call them. I just can't." He gave his mother a wild look and then bolted from the room.

"Justin!" Marcia was sitting up in the bed now, the dark circles under her eyes even more pronounced.

"I'll go after him." James fled the room before he was even sure it was the right thing to do. Justin wasn't anywhere in sight. He probably hadn't taken the elevators. James rushed past the nurse's station and glanced at Barbara who was pointing down the hall toward the stairwell, but as he rushed through the fire door he heard a door slam shut below, probably on the first floor. James hurried down the stairs, wincing as his knees protested.

He turned the corner at the landing and kept up his pounding descent, but when he reached the first floor, there was no sight of Justin to either the left or the right. James hurried toward the main entrance of the hospital and out the double doors, glancing up and down the sidewalk. Justin was nowhere in sight. James headed back into the hospital and onto the elevator.

Gideon stood as James entered Marcia's room. The woman's eyes were closed but her face looked far from peaceful.

"She called her parents—they weren't home," Gideon said. "Then the nurse gave her something and she fell asleep. Did you find him?"

"No. Any idea where he would go?"

Gideon stepped toward the door. "No."

"Let's go home," James said, leading the way down the hall. As they waited for the elevator, he remembered that he'd forgotten his travel mug in the staff lounge. "I'll meet you downstairs," he said to Gideon.

Ten minutes later with his coffee cup in hand, the elevator door opened and James searched the lobby for Gideon but didn't see him. Out of the corner of his eye, he spotted a police cruiser parked in front. James hurried off the elevator. Cesar stood beside it, talking into his radio.

James stopped at the receptionist desk. "What's going on?" he asked.

"The vandal struck again," the woman said. "In broad daylight."

"What happened?"

"Tagged the fence around the courtyard."

"Oh," James said, his mouth suddenly dry. He scanned the lobby again for Gideon and then headed through the sliding glass doors for the second time in twenty minutes.

Gideon wasn't in front of the hospital either or near the courtyard fence. James jogged toward the van, squinting in the afternoon light to see if Gideon was sitting in the passenger seat. He couldn't tell until he was within ten feet of the vehicle. Gideon was there, his head back against the seat, his eyes closed. James took a deep breath and opened the driver's side, hoping Justin was in the van too. He wasn't. "Gid," James said.

His son opened his eyes and shifted his head.

"Have you been in here the whole time?"

Gideon nodded.

"Seen Justin anywhere?"

Gideon shook his head and yawned.

"Did you see anything?"

"I was sleeping."

James concentrated on his son for a long moment. Was his boy telling the truth? "The vandal struck again," James said. "Tagged the courtyard fence." He looked for a reaction but there wasn't one.

Gideon sat up straight and his face reddened. "And you think Justin did it?"

"No." James looked around. "I'm not saying that—I just wondered if you saw anything. But speaking of Justin, we need to find him. He can't stay by himself another night."

They stopped by the Barneses' home, but no one answered their knocks on the door. Next they drove by the school and then to the park, but there was no sign of Justin.

"We should have asked him to stay with us from the beginning." Gideon's arms were crossed tightly across his chest as James pulled into the driveway of their house.

James decided not to respond. In retrospect, he acknowledged that's what he should have done. But hindsight was 20/20; and sometimes, with trying to juggle caring for Fern, work, the boys, and everything else, it was hard for him to know exactly how much he could handle.

Chapter Twelve

S ANABELLE LEFT REPORT FRIDAY MORNING, SHE sighed. She was tired. It had been a long, hard week. That was probably why she was feeling emotional, plus Ainslee hadn't returned her phone call or stopped by. She wanted more than anything to have a good relationship with her daughter and coming grandchild.

She headed for Marcia's room. The woman was too weak and still in too much pain to be transferred. The stress test had been inconclusive and her recovery was definitely slow, one of the slowest Anabelle had seen. Dr. Hildebrand was still sorting out her medications.

Anabelle heard voices as she approached the door and realized it was Janice speaking with Marcia. "I double-checked with your parents," Janice said, "and they're on their way. They'll take Justin home with them this weekend. I left a message with the school to have Justin come here right after class."

"Thank you."

Anabelle stepped all the way into the room and said hello. Both women acknowledged her and then continued speaking.

"I don't know where he's stayed all week," Marcia said.

"Where do you think he did?" Janice asked.

"At our house, most likely."

"And last night too?"

Marcia nodded.

"That's what I've surmised too," Janice said. "He didn't stay with the Bells, and Gideon didn't have any contact with him after he left the hospital."

Anabelle checked Marcia's IV.

"Speaking of your house," Janice continued. "The electricity will be turned back on Monday. And," she glanced down at her notes. "I couldn't locate a landline for your husband's friend, but I did come up with an address. A Chicago social worker will deliver a note asking your husband to contact the hospital."

"Thank you." Marcia's voice was low.

As Janice left the room, Anabelle charted the dose of morphine.

"I wonder if she knows I was once quite capable of taking care of my family," Marcia whispered.

"Pardon?" Anabelle stepped closer to the bed.

"The social worker. She treats me like a child."

Anabelle patted Marcia's foot. She could see why the woman felt that way, but Anabelle had seen Janice in action long enough to know that she treated everyone in the same professional manner. Obviously Marcia was feeling down—in more ways than one.

Anabelle sat at the nurses' station after reporting to the swing shift, reconciling the medication list when James leaned against the counter. "I had a text from Gideon that Justin's at school today."

"Oh, good," Anabelle said. "At least he's okay."

"Any word on the vandal?"

Anabelle slipped her reading glasses from her face. "I talked with Cesar this morning. They still don't have any leads—but an analyst came out from Peoria and went through the files and photos. He thinks it's from the same can of paint as the previous tags."

James grimaced. All of the nurses at the hospital were disgusted by the vandalism. It was insulting to think that someone in Deerford could do such a thing.

"Well, I'm headed home." James stood up straight. "Have a good weekend."

As James walked down the hall, Anabelle replaced her reading glasses on her nose and returned her attention to finishing the med list.

"Anabelle?" Janice stood in front of her.

"I'm sorry—I didn't even hear you." Anabelle put her pen down on the schedule. "What do you need?"

"Marcia's parents are here. And Justin. Do you mind coming into her room?" Janice practically whispered.

"Sure." Anabelle tucked her glasses into the pocket of her lab coat and followed the social worker into Marcia's room. Justin stood next to his mom's bed, his arms crossed and the hood of his sweatshirt pulled tight. An older man with a cane sat in the chair staring at the linoleum, and a sweet-looking woman with short curly gray hair stood at the end of the bed, staring at Marcia. The room was thick with tension.

"This is Anabelle Scott," Janice said, looking first at the woman and then the man. "She's the day charge nurse of the Cardiac Care Unit. Anabelle, this is Mr. and Mrs. Williams. Marcia's parents."

"We asked to see the doctor." The man's voice was gruff and he didn't raise his head.

"The doctor isn't available," Janice said. "She's seeing patients at her office. Anabelle can answer your questions."

The older woman cleared her throat and Anabelle turned toward her. "When will Marcia be discharged?"

"Not for two or three more days. She's still weak and in a lot of pain, and we're trying to address her abnormal heart rhythms."

"When Bud"—she nodded toward her husband—"had his heart attack, he was out in no time."

"Each case is different," Anabelle said. "Marcia's heart is still healing, and we've just started her on a new medication that seems to be working—but we need to give her a couple more days." She forced herself to exhale and inhale slowly.

"We were hoping to take her with us. Get her away from here before that no-good husband of hers returns." The man raised his head this time, showing a square, determined jaw.

Justin's hand clenched into a fist and Marcia reached for it, stroking it open.

"No," Anabelle said firmly. "Marcia has to remain in the hospital. No one here would discharge her yet, not in the condition she's in."

"I see," Mrs. Williams said. "Well, we'll just take Justin then." Justin shook his head.

"Justin, please go with them. It's just for the weekend. Dad will be back soon," Marcia said. "Then you can stay at the house with him."

A frown spread across Mrs. William's face. "Justin can stay with us as long as he needs."

"Please bring him back Monday morning in time for school." Marcia winced as she sat up straighter. "If Dan isn't home, I'll ask Gideon's father if he can stay there." She squeezed Justin's hand. "Call me every night before you go to bed."

Justin nodded, but his face was still contorted.

"Do you promise?" Marcia asked.

He softened a little and then bent down and kissed his mother's forehead. A second later he stumbled from the room. Neither of Marcia's parents hugged her or kissed her. They simply followed after Justin.

Marcia slumped down in the bed and pushed the button on the side. The bed began to lower. Janice began to speak but Marcia cut her off. "Please," she said. "I'm exhausted."

Anabelle followed Janice out into the hall. "How can we help her if she won't tell us what's really going on?"

"It's a typical response." The social worker clutched her clipboard against her chest. "Sometimes it takes people a while to feel safe enough to tell. Or they have to hit bottom first."

"A major heart attack isn't bottom?" Anabelle knew the social worker was right, even though she wanted to hold onto her expectations about how people should act.

Janice shrugged. "Not always." She took a step down the hall and then said, "Could you make a note to alert security and the social worker on duty if her husband does appear?" Janice asked.

"I already have," Anabelle said. She'd have to concentrate on acting in a professional manner if Marcia's husband did show up.

As she walked to her car, thoughts of Marcia, her parents, and Justin all bounced around in Anabelle's head. She couldn't imagine the awful tension between Marcia and her parents. She shivered as she reached the car. But here she was, sort of separated from Ainslee right now. At least it felt that way.

A few minutes later she drove her Ford Fusion down Cahokia Avenue toward her home, but when she reached Rishell Street she turned right instead of left, heading toward the Deerford square. She had her quilting group in a few days, and she'd seen a quilt in a magazine a few weeks ago that was made from old aprons and dishtowels. It would look perfect on the window seat in her kitchen. She knew Once Upon A Time had the old aprons, and she wouldn't be surprised if they had dishtowels too. She had thought it wasn't right to cut up an old apron but the example in the magazine had been darling.

She wasn't even sure if Ainslee was working, so it wasn't like she was stopping by to check on her. Not really.

Anabelle paused a moment in the crisp spring air and forced herself to smile, hoping it would make her appear more relaxed, and then pushed the door open, activating the chimes.

She craned her neck toward the back of the shop where the register was, but she didn't see anyone. Ainslee's car wasn't parked out front but maybe there was employee parking in the back. She wasn't sure. She headed to the apron rack and began fingering the fabric of a yellow-print smock. It was worn and soft and reminded Anabelle of her grandmother's kitchen outside Peoria all those years ago. She lifted the garment to her face and inhaled.

"Mother." Ainslee stood a few feet away with her arms crossed. "What are you doing?"

Anabelle dropped the apron. "Remembering." She stood up straight. "How are you?"

"Fine." Ainslee's hair hung loose around her shoulders, and she wore a green dress with tights and flats. Her belly looked much larger than it had last time she had seen her.

"I'm looking for old aprons and dishtowels. I'm thinking about making a lap quilt for the window seat." Anabelle turned her attention to a baby blue apron.

"Has Elena called you about the shower?"

"She left a message."

Anabelle ran her finger over the row of buttons on the bib of the apron. That meant Ainslee hadn't called her back.

"Mother, could you really cut up such a sweet piece of history?" Ainslee wasn't smiling. "The apron is perfect the way it is."

"Well, sure. But I'd be recycling it. Right?"

"Why don't you just buy the fabric?"

Anabelle shrugged. "I'm going to ask Kirstie and Evan to come over for dinner after church on Sunday. Would you like to join us?"

"I'll talk to Doug about it."

Anabelle pulled the yellow apron and the blue one from the rack.

Ainslee put her hand out for the aprons. "I'll put these by the register for you."

"Thanks, sweetie."

Ainslee headed to the register as Anabelle walked across the store, fighting the sinking feeling that was about to consume her daughter. Suddenly she wanted nothing more than to be home with Cameron.

She turned toward the register. "That's all the shopping I'm going to do today," she said. "I'll buy the aprons and think about the dishtowels—whether I really do want to desecrate history to make a quilt." She tried to smile.

"Are you all right?" Ainslee actually looked concerned.

"I'm tired, that's all. It's been a long week at work."

"Oh." Ainslee rang up the aprons and Anabelle paid. "I'll call you after I talk to Doug," Ainslee said as she handed her the bag. She made eye contact with her mother and said sweetly, "Thank you."

"For?" Anabelle dangled the bag at her side.

"For shopping at Once Upon A Time." Her green eyes sparkled.

"You're welcome." Anabelle felt a little lost at being treated like a customer instead of a mother as she left the shop and stepped out into the spring sunshine. As she neared her car,

Heather Miller approached wearing a short skirt, fashion boots, and a long black sweater. She held a stack of papers in her hand.

"How are you, Heather?" Anabelle asked.

Heather squinted. "Oh, hi." She lifted the papers. "Fine. Just out pounding the pavement, putting in résumés at all the restaurants. I'm hoping to be able to pretend to be a sous chef."

"Good for you," Anabelle said. "Something will turn up."

Heather made a face.

"How's your dad doing?"

The girl shrugged. "He won't listen to me about seeing a doctor in Springfield. He can be so stubborn." She waved as she stepped ahead. "Gotta go—even though it probably won't do me any good."

Chapter Thirteen

ANABELLE STOOD AT HER KITCHEN WINDOW, holding the phone to her ear.

"How about coffee?" Elena asked. "I have Izzy this morning."

"I was going to go into Princeton to look for fabric."

"Ooh, that sounds like fun!" Elena said. "I need some too."

It was Saturday morning and Anabelle hadn't been able to sleep in past six thirty. Now it was almost ten thirty.

"We can get lunch," Elena added. "I'll drive since I already have Izzy's booster seat in my Jeep."

Anabelle agreed, and Elena said she would be right over. Anabelle didn't feel like very good company, but she knew spending time with Elena and Izzy would cheer her up. Besides, Cameron was helping Evan with a design project and wouldn't be home for several hours, and she'd been slipping more and more into a funk as the morning dragged along. She needed to grocery shop for tomorrow's dinner—Evan and Kirstie both said they could come—but besides that, her day was wide open, and she'd been moping around obsessing about Ainslee who hadn't given her an answer about the dinner yet. A trip to Princeton with Elena, and sweet little Izzy, would do her good.

She tucked the phone into the pocket of her sweatshirt, stepped outside, and filled Sarge's dish with water. The puppy barked and wagged his tail, brushing up against Anabelle. She bent down and scratched his head. "You're on your own for a while," she said.

Ten minutes later, Elena arrived and Anabelle headed out in the drizzling rain, checking her cell as she did. She had a text from Ainslee. "Yes on dinner after church." That was all. Anabelle answered, "See you then," and slipped her phone into her purse.

"*Hola, bella* Isabella," she said, climbing into the passenger seat, her head turned toward the back. "How are you?"

The little girl giggled. "Hi, Aunt Amabelle," Izzy said, mispronouncing Anabelle's name as she always did. Izzy had her grandmother's caramel skin, but her eyes were gray. Their hair was nearly the same black, but Elena's was straight while Izzy's was a cascade of long, long curls.

"How's the grandmother-to-be?" Elena asked. She looked younger than she did at work with her hair fanned over her shoulders.

"Good." Anabelle turned her attention to her friend. "Did Ainslee call?"

"She left a message." Elena backed out of the driveway. "But I haven't heard back from her again. I'm thinking, at this point, we'll have the shower after the baby's born."

Anabelle relaxed against the seat, grateful that Elena was hosting the celebration. Maybe it was what she and Ainslee needed to smooth things over.

Elena turned onto the highway as Izzy called out, "Aunt Amabelle, look at Oinky." She held up a tattered pink pig. "She flies." Izzy zoomed the stuffed animal around the backseat, giggling as she did.

"What an amazing pig," Anabelle said, shifting in her seat. It wasn't the first time she'd met Oinky. "Can she talk?"

"She just says 'oink, oink.'" Isabella snorted after she spoke and then laughed again. "That's how she got her name."

"Wow—a pig that can fly and who named herself. She's remarkable." Anabelle turned back toward Elena and said, "She's so much fun."

Elena smiled as she accelerated down the highway. "I can't imagine my life without her." Elena's voice was quiet and Anabelle could barely hear her over Izzy's oinking.

Anabelle glanced over her shoulder. The little girl tapped the pig's nose against the window and continued oinking.

"Just wait," Elena said. "Being a grandmother is the best. Everything is more relaxed. I can see the bigger picture. I play with her more. Teach her." Elena's voice was still low. "I simply enjoy her."

Anabelle smiled.

"That's why I want to give Ainslee and you a shower," Elena said. "Because, sure, life is going to change for Ainslee, but it's going to change for you too."

"Thank you," Anabelle said.

"I'm just so excited for you." Elena reached over and squeezed Anabelle's hand. "So, are things better with her?"

"All the kids are coming over for dinner tomorrow after church."

"Excellent," Elena said.

"But I'm not so sure." Anabelle didn't want to talk about Ainslee not wanting her at the birth, but she did want Elena to know things weren't going smoothly. "Ainslee is still acting like she's really annoyed with me."

Elena laughed. "Like she's in high school again?"

"Kind of."

"Well, remember how many hormones she has coursing through her body right now—plus all the anxiety of being a new mom."

Anabelle reminded herself of both things several times a day. "She says I stress her out. That I'm too critical of her."

"Really?"

Anabelle nodded.

Elena passed a tractor. "Maybe Ainslee is having a confidence crisis."

"Maybe."

"What can we do to give Ainslee a boost?" Elena tapped her thumb on the steering wheel as she pulled back into her lane.

Anabelle noticed she still had her purse in her lap and that she was clutching it. She slipped it down to the floor. She hadn't thought about trying to make Ainslee feel better about being a mom. "I don't know," she said. "Do you have any ideas?"

Elena tossed her hair off her shoulder. "Well, we don't want to play any of those silly games at the shower. You know. The ones where everyone shares the worst birth story ever or how hard babies are or why they wish they'd never had kids."

Anabelle knew exactly what Elena was talking about. She also knew that making Ainslee feel like she would be a good mom wasn't going to happen at the shower. It had to happen before then. And Anabelle had to be subtle about it, otherwise Ainslee would feel like she was being patronized. Ainslee probably had no idea that being a mother wasn't always easy for Anabelle, that there were times when she felt like the worst mother ever, but she always kept trying, always kept moving forward.

"As nurses, we have a little bit of an advantage when it comes to being a mom." Elena was still talking. "We know how to bathe and bundle a baby, and we know about jaundice and burping. All that stuff we learned in our Pediatrics rotation."

Anabelle chuckled. "Right. All that easy stuff."

"Exactly," Elena said. "Babies." She looked into the rearview mirror. "And five-year-olds." She sighed. "If only they stayed so easy. Maybe I'll have everyone share their best parenting advice at the shower." Elena laughed.

The conversation turned to Hope Haven and the recent vandalism. Elena had heard that five hundred dollars had been raised for the stained-glass window, but that it was just a drop in the bucket. Much more was needed. Both women shook their heads in dismay.

Next the conversation turned to sewing, with the women turning their attention to Izzy now and then, until they reached Princeton. They stopped on the outskirts of town at the strip mall and headed into the fabric store. As they reached the front door, Elena bent down, balancing on her three-inch-heeled boots, and spoke softly to Izzy. "Remember, we use our inside voices and hands."

"I won't touch a thing," Izzy said, stuffing her hands into the pockets of her pink fleece jacket.

Elena gave her a hug and stood gracefully.

Anabelle swallowed the lump in her throat. She wanted—more than anything—to have a good relationship with her grandchild.

On the way to lunch, Elena wound through the old, tree-lined streets of the town. Grand homes built in the 1800s graced the neighborhood, houses with wide porches, turrets, and widows' walks on the roofs. "I was thinking about making Izzy a bonnet," Elena said. "And maybe an old-fashioned dress too."

Anabelle glanced behind her. Oinky was kissing the window again.

"You know," Elena said, "the thing with being a grandparent is that it changes everything. All of a sudden you're bowing to your kids to keep the peace, not offering advice when you would have before. All of that."

"Even though you help with Izzy so much?"

"Even though." Elena turned onto Main Street and parked in front of the Italian restaurant in an old brick building.

"*Buela*," Izzy said, calling Elena by the name she used for her grandmother. "I'm hungry."

"Good, sweetie, because it's time to eat," Elena answered as Anabelle's phone rang.

She checked the screen. "It's Ainslee."

"Go ahead. Izzy and I will go use the restroom."

Anabelle answered her phone with a sweet hello. Ainslee jumped right in. "Elena wants to set the date for the shower. She mentioned April twenty-fourth before—that works for me."

"That hardly gives Elena time to send out the invitations." It was only a week away.

"Mother, Elena's the one who suggested it. And I really want to have the shower before the baby's born."

With all of her resolve, Anabelle willed herself to bite her tongue and let Elena work out the details with Ainslee.

Chapter Fourteen

CANDACE SAT AT THE NURSES' STATION SATURDAY night because the charge nurse for the night shift had called in sick, and the head nurse of the unit had begged Candace to fill in. It wasn't often she worked weekends—or nights—but she'd decided to take a turn. She double-checked her patient's chart. Forty-one. Primigravida. Breech. Definitely high risk. She called down to radiology and put in an order for an ultrasound. The woman thought the baby had flipped, but it needed to be confirmed. If it hadn't, a cesarean was inevitable.

When Candace reentered the birthing room, the woman was standing and her husband was rubbing her lower back. "How are you doing?" Candace asked, approaching the couple slowly.

"Good." The woman's name was Sally, and she grimaced as a contraction overtook her. Sweat beaded on her forehead and her face grew red.

Candace counted silently and reached seventy-three by the time the woman started breathing normally again.

"That was intense," her husband Paul said, pushing his wire-rim glasses back onto his nose. His temples were gray and his forehead wrinkled.

The woman nodded.

"You're doing great," Candace said sincerely, glancing at the baby monitor. The heartbeat was strong. A decision needed to be made soon about whether a C-section needed to be done or not.

"A tech will be in soon to do an ultrasound, to check the position of the baby."

"I'm sure he flipped," Sally said, half sitting on the edge of the bed, her gown sticking straight out over her belly. "It was like a wave—right honey?"

Paul nodded.

"Okay, but we have to confirm the position. I'll be right back." She'd had patients before who had been sure a baby had changed positions and had been wrong. Candace hurried out of the room and checked on her second patient. Thankfully she was hours away from delivery. She showed the woman's husband how to massage her back with tennis balls and told them to buzz her if they needed anything. As she stepped back into the hall, Heath Carlson pushed an ultrasound cart down the corridor toward her.

"Hi," Candace said, her heart fluttering a little at the surprise of seeing him.

"You called?" Heath smiled and Candace's eyes were drawn to his dimples.

"I didn't expect you." He was a shift supervisor, usually day shift, and he specialized in MRIs. He must have been called in tonight too.

"We're shorthanded," he said, and then smiled again. His golden hair was a little longer than he usually wore it, and it was curling around his ears.

"So are we." Candace led the way into the room and introduced Heath to the couple.

"How are you doing?" Heath asked the woman.

"Okay." She smiled.

The husband took his wife's hand and squeezed it.

Candace felt the patient's abdomen and thought that the baby might have flipped too, but the baby was so low that it was impossible to tell for sure.

Heath asked the woman to recline on the bed as he plugged in the machine, chatting as he worked. "How long have you lived in Deerford?" he asked the couple.

"Five years," the husband answered.

"We've been hoping for a baby the entire time." The woman tucked the pillow beneath her head. "And here we are!"

Candace smiled. The couple was as cute as could be.

Heath stepped toward the bed with the ultrasound wand in his hand. "I'm assuming that you've had one of these done," he said.

The woman nodded. "And we already know it's a boy, so no need to keep it a secret."

"The heartbeat is nice and strong," Heath said as he moved the wand around. He stopped grinning. "There's the foot." He pointed to the screen. He didn't have to say the baby was still breech; it was obvious to all of them.

"I'll call Dr. Carpenter." Candace patted Sally's shoulder.

Her husband took her hand. "A healthy baby is what counts."

Candace slipped out of the room. A couple of minutes later she hung up the phone and nearly bumped into Heath as he came out of Sally's room, pushing the cart again. She blushed and thanked him for his help.

"This is the best of the best," Heath said. "As far as work."

She smiled.

He blushed. "I mean, *you* get to be around this every day, but for me, it's a thrill."

"It's still a thrill for me," Candace said. "And I pray it always will be."

A beat of silence passed between them. "Hey, I was planning on heading to the cafeteria in a bit. Would you like to meet me there?"

"Sure."

"Let's say twenty minutes."

Candace smiled and nodded.

Twenty minutes later, Candace sat at the far table in the cafeteria sipping her coffee and skimming the for-sale ads in the *Hope Haven Newsletter* as she waited for Heath. Someone was selling a tent, camping stove, and a canoe. Dean had been an avid outdoorsman, but she hadn't taken the kids camping since he'd died. She couldn't remember if she still had Dean's old tent or not—hopefully it was still in the garage.

"Hey, there." Heath stood next to the table holding a paper cup with the string of a tea bag hanging halfway down the side.

Candace's eyes met his and her heart fluttered for the second time that night.

He slid into the opposite side of the booth. "Are you doing some shopping?" he asked, nodding toward the newsletter.

"Just browsing." She chuckled. "Actually, I was just wondering if I could take the kids camping by myself."

Heath tilted his head.

"I doubt if Mom would want to go. She's a city girl at heart."

"Do you have the equipment?" Heath asked.

"I think so." Candace sighed. "Howie has been pretty active lately though—I'd have to make sure he took the whole thing seriously—the not wandering off part, all of that."

Heath bobbed his tea bag up and down in his cup. "How's the little champ?"

Candace explained what the teacher had said and that the specialist had written out a prescription.

"Have you gotten it filled?" Heath asked.

"Not yet."

"How come?"

Candace exhaled slowly. "I'm not sure it's the right thing for Howie." She'd been online, researching the medication. She wasn't sure if his problems were extreme enough to warrant chancing any of the most extreme side effects.

Heath leaned across the table and then whispered, "My teacher told my mom I was hyper when I was in the third grade." He said it as if it were top secret and then broke out into a grin.

"What happened?" Candace asked.

He leaned back and resumed a normal voice. "The teacher was right—I was a handful. My dad decided what I needed was to learn discipline and respect, so he signed me up for karate lessons."

"Really?"

"Plus he sent me outside to play for two hours every day after school when I didn't have karate."

Candace thought of Howie playing with Legos and watching cooking shows with Brooke after school. He'd played soccer in the fall but hadn't been active through the winter. "That's a great idea," she said. Maybe he didn't have ADD—maybe he simply needed to wear himself out.

"There are a couple of karate clubs in town." Heath wrapped his hands around his paper cup. "One out on the highway."

Candace nodded. She knew the place.

"And one at the Methodist Church."

"Really?" She had no idea that churches hosted karate clubs.

Heath nodded. "I don't know much about the program though. I only made it to a red belt—I stopped when I was in junior high for Boy Scouts."

Candace leaned forward and whispered. "So, I'm assuming you were no longer hyper by then."

Heath laughed. "Your assumptions are correct. By then I was a full-fledged nerd."

Candace glanced at the clock above the door. It was seven thirty. "I'd better get going." Dr. Carpenter would be arriving any minute.

Heath slipped out of the booth as she did and said, "I'll say a prayer for the mother and baby—and the dad."

Candace appreciated his concern.

Heath waved and headed for the imaging department.

Candace decided to take the stairs. As she climbed, she hoped that rigorous activity was what Howie needed. She slowed as she reached the door. On the other hand, she didn't want to deny the fact that Howie might fit the ADD diagnosis. Denial wouldn't do any of them any good either.

Chapter Fifteen

LET'S GO," ANABELLE SAID TO CAMERON, CATCHING his hand as they walked from the sanctuary of the Church of the Good Shepherd and into the sea of people milling around the foyer.

Cameron tilted his head. "What's the hurry?"

"The kids are coming over. Remember?" Anabelle dropped Cameron's hand and slipped into her coat. She'd started a roast before they left for church and didn't want it to dry out before it was time to eat.

"Anabelle!" It was Fern Bell, leaning against her walker with Nelson at her side.

"Fern!" Anabelle wound her way around a group of people and greeted her friend with a hug. "How are you?"

"Just fine," Fern answered.

Anabelle gave Nelson a half hug and asked him how school was going.

"Good," he answered.

Anabelle turned back to Fern. "You look good." She stood straighter than usual and had more color in her face.

"The doctor started me on some new medication, a shot. It seems to be helping."

"Do you give yourself the injections?"

Fern shook her head. "James does."

"Well, you're lucky."

Fern nodded. "I certainly am."

James stood a few feet away from the women, talking to Cameron. In the distance, Ainslee and Doug started down the hallway to the back exit.

"It's good to see you." Anabelle gave Fern another hug and then stepped toward Cameron, reaching for his hand. "We need to get going," she whispered.

He shot her an amused look, so she confided to James, "Our kids are all coming for Sunday dinner."

"Wonderful," James said.

"See you tomorrow at work," Anabelle said as she waved to the Bells, not wanting Ainslee to reach the house first. The service had gone a little late. Perhaps Kirstie and Evan would beat them home too.

As they hurried out the front double doors of the church, the warm day enveloped them. Overnight, it had turned to spring. A robin hopped around on the strip of grass between the parking lot and the sidewalk, and the pink petals of the flowering cherry trees floated back and forth with the breeze. It was a great time of year for Ainslee's baby to be born. They would be able to get out of the house and go for walks, even go to the park as soon as possible. Anabelle increased her pace as she imagined walking with them, maybe pushing the stroller or carrying the baby.

Cameron chuckled as he struggled to keep up with her. "You'd think the queen was coming to dinner."

Anabelle slowed. She did feel like a queen was coming over, Queen Ainslee. They reached the car and climbed in, yanking the doors shut in unison.

"When did you start giving our children so much power?" Cameron asked, as he turned out of the church parking lot.

Anabelle sat tall in the bucket seat of the car. "What do you mean?"

"You seem worried about what the kids will think. It's as if you need to please them or something."

"Not all of them."

"You're right. Not Evan. Or Kirstie," Cameron said, turning onto Rishell Street. "Just Ainslee."

Anabelle didn't answer.

"Annie?"

"I heard." She hadn't thought about wanting to please Ainslee, but she did feel as if she were walking on eggshells.

"Why?" Cameron said. "Do you think she'll change her mind about maybe not wanting you at the birth?"

"It's not about the birth." Anabelle's voice was soft. Although it was distressing that Ainslee had said she wasn't sure she wanted Anabelle with her when the baby arrived, Anabelle hadn't breathed another word about it to her daughter. Hadn't asked even when she longed to. But not being at the birth wasn't her biggest worry, not now. Her biggest fear was that Ainslee would have the baby and not want Anabelle involved.

She thought of Elena and Isabel and all the fun they had together. Anabelle couldn't bear the thought of having a grandchild and not being allowed to have a close relationship with him or her. And no matter what, she wouldn't bring up the date of the shower. Elena had assured her that it was no problem to put it together in a week. She had planned to call all of the guests last evening and then get the invitations in the mail by Monday morning.

"Annie?"

Anabelle looked down at her lap. "I just want things to go well, that's all."

"What's not to go well? You scrubbed the house from top to bottom yesterday afternoon. And you've been cooking since dawn." He slowed as the car approached their driveway.

"Oh no," Anabelle said. Ainslee and Doug were climbing from their car.

Cameron shook his head but didn't say anything.

She'd wanted to arrive first and have a few minutes to get organized, but Ainslee's obsessive punctuality had won. Actually, she'd most likely gotten the always-be-on-time habit from Anabelle.

Cameron hit the garage opener on the driver's visor, and then pulled ahead into the garage and left the door up for Ainslee and Doug.

Anabelle forced a cheery, "Hello," as she climbed from the car.

Cameron gave Ainslee a hug and then shook Doug's hand as Anabelle hurried into the kitchen. Cameron was right; she was much too uptight about the dinner. They'd had the kids all over oodles of times since they'd all moved out, and she'd never been anxious about it before.

The hearty scent of the roast met her as she hung up her coat, but when she opened the oven and took the foil off the cut of meat it looked a little overdone. She thrust a fork in a potato wedge; it was softer than she liked. She turned off the oven and scanned the kitchen and then the dining room. She had set the table before she left and made the salad, but she still needed to make the gravy.

Cameron came through the door, followed by Doug and then Ainslee. "Mother, can I help?" her daughter asked, slipping out of her jacket.

"No, no," Anabelle replied, tying the blue apron from Once Upon A Time—she'd decided to use them instead of cut them into quilting squares—over her dress, feeling very much like a grandmother. "You go rest." She turned toward the cupboard and took out a glass. "Would you like something to drink? Juice? Milk? Water?"

Ainslee shook her head. "I can set . . . " Her voice trailed off as she looked into the dining room. "Never mind."

"Just go rest," Anabelle said. "I'll let you know if I need any help in a few minutes." It usually didn't make her nervous to have people hang out in her kitchen—especially not her daughters—but she was afraid of saying the wrong thing to Ainslee, of setting her daughter off again. She hoped the other kids would arrive soon. She was less likely to say something offensive—or maybe it was that Ainslee was less likely to get offended—if others were around.

Evan arrived as Anabelle stirred cornstarch into the roast drippings and beef broth.

He bent down to kiss her cheek, his dark red hair pushed back from his forehead.

"I didn't see you at church," she said.

"Are you checking up on me?"

She blushed.

He squeezed her shoulder. "I'm teasing. I was in the balcony—sitting with Kirstie."

"Is she here?" Anabelle pulled away from her son and glanced toward the back door.

"No. She went home to change."

Anabelle returned to stirring the gravy. "Dad, Ains, and Doug are in the living room."

"Do you need any help?" Evan asked.

"Would you ask everyone what they want to drink?"

Evan nodded and then lifted the cake pan lid. "*Hmm,*" he said. "German chocolate cake. My favorite."

Anabelle smiled. It was Ainslee's favorite too. It had been their grandmother's recipe.

A few minutes later, as Evan poured the drinks, Anabelle turned the heat under the gravy down, feeling pleased. She would dish up as soon as Kirstie arrived. So far so good.

Twenty minutes later, she called Kirstie's cell phone but it went straight to voice mail. She left a terse, "Where are you?" message and then turned to Evan who had wandered back into the kitchen. "She said she was coming—right?"

He nodded.

"Well, I'm going to go ahead and dish up. I bet Ainslee's starving."

Evan grabbed a celery stick from the platter on the counter and plunged it into the ranch dressing. "Actually, she seems fine," he said and then took a bite, the crunch echoing across the kitchen.

"Why don't you take the veggie plate into the living room?" Anabelle asked. "Tell the others we'll sit down in a few minutes." She opened the oven and took out the roast, using the meat fork to lift it onto the cutting board. She began slicing it, frowning a little at how done it was. She would serve the middle portion and save the ends for leftovers for her and Cameron.

A few minutes later, as she covered the roast with foil, Kirstie came through the back door.

"Where have you been?" Anabelle didn't mean to sound exasperated but it showed in her tone.

"At my apartment changing. Didn't Evan tell you?"

Anabelle nodded. "I just didn't think it would take so long."

Kirstie's dark hair was pulled back in a ponytail and she wore jeans and a cotton sweater. "It's so nice out, I almost walked over—but I thought that would really stress you out." She smiled and hugged her mother, bumping against her shin. Anabelle could feel the hard plastic of her daughter's prosthesis.

"Has Ainslee found out if the baby is a girl or boy yet?" Kirstie asked, pulling away.

"I don't think so." Anabelle couldn't think of any reason that Ainslee would have had another ultrasound, but frankly, even if Ainslee did know the gender of the baby, she wouldn't expect her to reveal it.

Kirstie crossed her arms. "It's ridiculous that they don't want to know. Don't you think?"

Anabelle shook her head. "I think it's sweet." She was sure the baby was a girl; Ainslee was carrying the baby high and she still craved chocolate, two things Anabelle remembered well from when she was pregnant with her girls. Evan, on the other hand, was low the whole time and the thought of chocolate made her queasy.

"Well, I'd want to know. Someday, if I'm ever pregnant, I'm definitely finding out," Kirstie said.

Anabelle dished the potatoes and carrots into her china serving bowl. "Tell the others it's time to eat, would you please?"

As Kirstie headed to the living room, Anabelle hoped her youngest daughter would have children someday, once she married and settled down of course. She shook her head. Kirstie was private about her boyfriend, Mark Holcher, and Anabelle didn't think Kirstie had a wedding on the brain. There was no reason to think that far ahead. She needed to concentrate on now, on today, on how she could be supportive of Ainslee.

"Delicious," Cameron said. "As always." He pushed his chair back from the table just a little.

Doug dragged his roll across the smear of gravy left on his plate. "I agree." He made eye contract with Anabelle. "Thank you."

She acknowledged him with a nod and a smile.

"How about if we have dessert outside?" Evan said.

"Is there dessert?" Ainslee asked.

"German chocolate cake," Evan answered.

"With pecan topping?" she asked.

"Yep." Evan lifted his water glass.

Kirstie groaned. "Oh, I get it. This is like a special dinner for Ainslee, right? Because she's producing the first grandchild." She had a mischievous look on her face.

Evan began to laugh, but an anxious expression passed over Ainslee's face.

"I have peppermint ice cream in the freezer, Kirstie," Anabelle said. Her youngest had never liked chocolate cake. "And I think having dessert outside is a great idea." She stood and began to pick up the plates. "I'll go start a pot of decaf."

"Decaf," Kirstie protested. "Can't we have the real thing?"

"Okay, I'll make a pot of regular too."

Ainslee stood and picked up her plate and then Doug's.

"Oh, honey, you sit," Anabelle said. "I'll clear the table."

"Mother," Ainslee practically hissed. "Would you please stop treating me like an invalid?"

Kirstie snickered as Anabelle's face reddened.

"I'm pregnant—not ill." Ainslee turned and started toward the kitchen. Her maternity blouse was hitched up in the back along the elastic waistband of her pants and she waddled, just a little, as she walked. The rest of the family all paused for a second and then jumped to their feet, grabbing plates and dishes, napkins and cutlery.

A few minutes later Ainslee waddled through the door onto the patio as Doug threw a tennis ball for Sarge. Cameron and Evan huddled around the flowerbed in the corner of the yard, and Anabelle began to cut the cake.

Kirstie poured cups of decaf into blue mugs. "Have you seen Heather Miller around?"

"I did. I ran into her outside of Once Upon A Time a few days ago." In the old days Anabelle could reveal that she'd seen Heather at the hospital, but it was a different era now with all of the new standards on confidentiality.

"She had to drop out of culinary school."

"That's too bad," Anabelle said.

"Yeah. She was hoping to open a restaurant—probably not in Deerford though. She always hated it here. In fact, I heard she went to Springfield this weekend for a job interview." Kirstie turned toward the sliding door. "I'm going to go check on the real coffee."

Ainslee settled into one of the patio chairs and yawned.

"Are you tired?" Anabelle asked.

"Mother," Ainslee said, pushing her hair from her eyes.

Anabelle winced and turned toward the men. "Time for dessert."

They all started toward the patio, but Evan and Cameron stopped for a moment to look at the rose bushes along the fence line.

"Who wants real coffee?" Kirstie called out as she came through the sliding glass door, holding a white carafe in one hand and a bowl of ice cream in the other.

"I do," Ainslee said, raising her hand as if she were in school.

"But you can't, right?" Anabelle interjected.

"Actually I can. I double-checked after our last conversation. The doctor said a cup or two a day is fine."

"Oh."

Doug stepped onto the patio. "It's true," he said. "I was there when she asked."

"But how can coffee possibly be good for the baby?" Anabelle caught Cameron's look of caution after she'd already spoken.

"It's fine." Ainslee poured cream into her cup. "Come out of the dark ages."

Kirstie and Evan chuckled, but Cameron said, "Mom's just looking out for everyone—like always."

"She doesn't need to look out for me," Ainslee said, wrapping her hand around her mug. "She thinks, just because she's a nurse, that she knows everything. I can read. I can ask questions."

Anabelle sat down as gracefully as she could, determined not to look hurt, and cut a bite of cake with her fork as an awkward silence fell over the group.

Finally, Kirstie raised a spoon of ice cream and said, "Hey Ains, I'm just happy she's hovering over you now instead of me."

Anabelle started to stand, but Evan jumped in. "Mother, the cake is delicious."

"Perfect as always." Cameron smiled at her.

Unable to speak, she nodded an acknowledgment, and as she did, a hummingbird darted across the patio and they all followed its flight over the fence and off into the pasture. After the excitement passed, Cameron and the children resumed their chatter, and no one seemed to notice that Anabelle remained silent.

Chapter Sixteen

UNDAY AFTERNOON, ELENA, WITH IZZY BY HER side, pushed the cart through the aisle of party supplies at the big box store on the edge of town. The previous evening, she had called everyone on the guest list, and they were all thrilled to save the date. Now she needed to get the invitations ready and in the mail by morning. Anabelle had been mortified that Ainslee put off scheduling the date of the shower and then suddenly decided April twenty-fourth would work after all. But Elena was fine with the way things had worked out. In fact, she had prepared herself for some last-minute drama.

"Let's get that!" Izzy pointed at an orange banner that featured two clowns and read, "Happy Birthday!" Izzy's head bobbed in her enthusiasm, and her pigtails swung back and forth.

"We're shopping for Ainslee and Aunt Anabelle's party." Elena squinted at the baby decorations. She hadn't found anything old-fashioned yet—and nothing close to sage. Everything was blue or pink.

"How about that?" Izzy pointed at a box of invitations with kittens on the front.

Elena suppressed a groan, imagining Ainslee's reaction. She wheeled the cart to the end of the aisle and paused for a moment. She didn't want to have to drive back to Princeton to find supplies for the shower, especially since she had just been there the day before. Ahead was the customer service kiosk. She pushed the cart toward it.

"I really liked the kitties." Izzy slumped and crossed her arms.

"I know, and for the right party, those would be perfect."

The young woman at the counter asked if she could help and then listened as Elena explained her problem. "I think we have sage-colored plates and napkins," the woman said. "Look in aisle ten." Then she lowered her voice. "As far as the other stuff, have you considered the craft store? You could buy paper and stamps in the scrapbooking section and make your own because, frankly, you're not going to find what you want here."

Elena thanked the young woman profusely. She hadn't thought of the craft store at the other end of town and wondered if she had the time—and creativity—to make the invitations.

Fifteen minutes later, she and Izzy stood in the scrapbooking section of the craft store.

"*Buela*, buy this stamp!" Izzy held a stamp of a puppy in her hand. "And this one!" She held up one of a pony.

Ainslee would have been thrilled with those when she was five too, Elena thought with a smile. "Put those back, please," she said. "And just look. Remember, no touching."

Izzy sighed and carefully placed the stamps back, then stood with her hands clasped behind her back.

"May I help you?" A young man wearing an apron approached. He appeared to be about seventeen and looked as if he belonged on a basketball court, not working in a craft store.

Elena explained her predicament. "The mother-to-be is very savvy and particular. She knows what she wants with regard to design and color and all of that."

He nodded and then turned toward the display of stamps. "Here's an old-fashioned buggy. You can use it on the invitations and then blow up an image of it for your centerpiece."

"What a great idea," Elena said. It wasn't like she was a stranger to design. She'd been making quilts for years. So why did she feel so nervous tackling this project? She supposed it had something to do with not wanting to disappoint the guest of honor.

At home, Elena stared at the supplies covering her kitchen table. The stamps—including the puppy one for Izzy—the ink pads, the note cards, the special pens, the sheets of scrapbooking paper were all arranged, ready to use. The young man had even shown her some quick embossing techniques, which she would use too.

"Let's get started," Izzy said, rubbing her hands together. Elena couldn't help but smile, wondering where Izzy had picked up the gesture. Her granddaughter beamed. She wasn't feeling apprehensive about the project, not one bit. And she was thrilled to spend a sunny afternoon working with paper and ink.

"*Buela?*" Izzy pushed up the sleeves of her shirt. "Are you going to stand there all day or get to work?"

Elena rubbed her hands together and took a deep breath. She could do it—for Ainslee and Anabelle, and for Izzy.

Two hours later, Elena thumbed through the stack of invitations. They were far from perfect. Most were smudged. Some were crooked. Izzy had smeared ink across a couple. Elena had put too much embossing powder on some and not enough on others. But all of them were endearing. She would save the best for Ainslee's baby book and mail out the rest. The baby was what mattered—not the centering on the invitations.

"We did good." Izzy looked up from the sheet of paper in front of her that she'd covered with puppies.

"We did, didn't we?" Elena stood and hugged her granddaughter. "Thank you so much for helping me."

"Brooke, you and Howie need to go outside to play." Candace stood in the doorway to the family room. "It's a beautiful day."

Brooke turned her head slowly from the TV. Her curly blonde hair fell over one eye.

"It's gorgeous today." At least it had been. Now it was late afternoon and growing colder.

"Can I finish my show?"

Howie didn't seem to hear Candace from the far corner where he sat surrounded by Legos.

"Howie," Candace said. "You and Brooke are going outside in a few minutes."

He nodded absently, and Candace headed back to the kitchen to finish cleaning out the refrigerator. Janet was out with Susan, looking at kitchen counters—Susan intended to remodel her kitchen sometime soon.

A pang of jealousy caught Candace off guard as she put a container of leftover spaghetti sauce on her worn Formica countertop. She chided herself. Self-pity would only pull her down; it wouldn't help her be the strong mother she wanted to be. She whispered a prayer of thanks for her house and children, for her mother's willingness to live with them, for her worn Formica, and all that she had. God met her needs.

After she cleared the refrigerator, she began wiping down the shelves, lost in her thoughts. A glance outside reminded her that the afternoon was growing late. "Brooke!" she called out. "Are you done with your show?"

"I started watching the next one," came the meek reply from the family room.

"Go outside now." Candace began arranging the condiments on the shelves of the door as she listened to Brooke tell her brother they were going to go play.

Howie's wail startled her. "But I don't want to."

Candace closed the door but before she could step out of the kitchen, Howie crashed against her legs and wrapped his arms around her thighs. "Brooke said I have to go outside."

"I said you have to go outside," Candace said. "It's warm out—you should have been out all afternoon."

"But I was playing Legos." His head was tipped back and his eyes were watery.

"Now it's time to play outside."

He stuck out his lower lip and then said, "Will you come with me?"

Candace turned toward the counters covered with food. It wouldn't hurt to leave it out for a little longer. "Sure," she said. "What do you want to do? Kick a soccer ball around?"

"Basketball." Howie let go of her legs and ran toward the front door.

She started to follow him down the hall but then stopped. "Brooke!" she called out. "Come on outside with us."

"I'll be there in a minute," she answered.

Candace slipped into her light jacket and grabbed the basketball from the box of sports equipment just inside the entryway, digging it out from under the kids' rollerblades. Howie led the way through the door, smiling back at her. Candace couldn't help but return his enthusiasm. She should have gone outside with him hours ago, when she first got up from her morning nap after the kids had returned from church with Mom. Why had she thought she needed to clean the fridge?

As Howie broke into a run, Candace followed, dribbling the ball as she did. She'd played basketball in junior high and enjoyed it.

Howie nearly tripped over his own feet as he reached the hoop.

"Careful," Candace called out and then wished she hadn't. She remembered reading several years ago about how differently mothers and fathers treated their children from the very beginning, starting with babies. Mothers held their infants close to them, with the baby's face against them in a position of protection, while fathers tended to hold babies face out so the children could see the world around them. Dean would never have told Howie to be careful.

Howie turned toward her, jumping up and down and waving his arms. "Pass me the ball!"

Candace bounced it off the pavement, gently, straight to him. He flung the ball up toward the basket but it didn't even reach the net. He grabbed the rebound and brought the ball down between his legs and then hurled it toward the basket, hitting the rim.

"Your turn!" Howie passed the ball to her.

Candace hopped a little as she released the ball and watched it sail toward the basket, bouncing off the backboard and down to the ground.

Howie clapped his hands together. "Great shot! Try it again." He grabbed the ball and passed it back to her.

As he passed the ball, their across-the-street neighbor and his son came out of their house, each bouncing a basketball.

"Hi," the man called out, and then spun a hook shot that swished through the net of the basketball hoop fixed over their garage.

"Wow." Howie stuffed his hands into his pockets.

Then the son, who was ten, shot from the middle of the driveway. It spun around the basket and then slipped in.

"Your turn," Candace said, bouncing the ball back to Howie.

He frowned and tried a shot like the older boy's but it arced well below the basket and bounced onto the lawn. Howie shuffled toward the ball, retrieved it, and bounce-passed it to Candace. He stood by the base of the hoop, staring across the street. The neighbors were playing a game of one-on-one. Howie sighed. "Can we go in now?" he asked.

"How about if we go for a walk around the block. We can take turns dribbling the ball."

"Okay," he said, a tone of reluctance in his voice. He took the ball and began slapping it.

"No, dribble it," Candace said, taking it from him. "Like this." She dribbled it carefully and slowly and then handed it back to him. He did a little better the second time but after about twenty feet it got away from him and bounced off his foot.

"I'll get it," Candace said.

"Can we go home?" Howie had both hands shoved in his pocket again. "I miss my Legos."

"Let's keep walking," Candace said. "Just once around the block."

When they reached the house, Janet's car was in the driveway, and the neighbors were still playing across the street. The dad had worked up a sweat and was wiping his face with the sleeve of his shirt. Howie stopped for a moment and stared as the man let his son by him, seemingly on purpose, and the boy made a layup. Howie's frown deepened and Candace let him lead the way into the house as she carried the ball up the walkway.

Candace closed the vegetable drawer of the refrigerator and then shut the door, thankful to have finished another chore on her to-do list.

"Maybe Howie would like to play basketball," Mom said as she leaned against the counter, a cup of herbal tea in her hand.

"I don't think they start until the second or third grade." Candace squirted soap onto her palm and scrubbed her hands. Brooke had never wanted to play, but Candace was sure the sport didn't start until later, surely not in kindergarten or even first grade. She turned the tap on. "I was thinking about karate."

"Karate?"

Candace looked over her shoulder.

Her mom had a confused look on her face. "As in breaking cement blocks with his bare hands?"

"I'm sure the younger kids don't do that." Candace almost laughed at the thought of Howie attacking a hunk of concrete.

"Oh." Janet took a sip of her tea. "Still," she said, "karate seems a little much, don't you think? What if it makes him aggressive on top of being active? Maybe you could just play basketball with him."

"Maybe." Candace turned the water off and dried her hands. The truth was, she was pretty sure she needed a program to keep Howie engaged and busy—and to keep the two of them from getting into a power play over being physically active.

"Did you get the prescription filled?" her mother asked.

Candace shook her head.

"Well, Susan and I were talking—"

Candace's face went slack. She hated it when her mother and Susan talked. She braced herself.

"And we were wondering if you could get a second opinion."

Candace took a deep breath and then exhaled slowly. That was better than she'd anticipated. "That's a good idea."

"Susan thought you might take him to his pediatrician to start with. Surely she could give you more information on the pros and cons of medication. That sort of thing."

Candace reached over and gave her mom a hug, careful not to bump her tea. "That's a great idea." *Why didn't I think of consulting with Dr. Amy?*

Janet put the cup of tea on the worn counter beside her and hugged Candace back. Then she sighed as she pulled away. "I actually don't know anything about karate." She smiled. "But I'll probably be learning about it soon if I know you."

"Probably." Candace grinned. She would stop by the Methodist Church and find out about the karate club. The sooner she enrolled Howie and gave it a try, the better.

Chapter Seventeen

"SO WE MEET AGAIN," ANABELLE CALLED OUT AS she slammed the driver's door to her Ford Fusion shut.

James smiled as he locked his van. "We can't seem to stay away from this place," he joked, stepping toward her. "How was your family dinner yesterday?"

"Good," Anabelle answered, not wanting to share her frustration with both herself and Ainslee. Here she'd wanted to encourage Ainslee and instead had created a bigger rift.

As they approached the entrance, Eddie Blaine came out the double doors, carrying pruning shears. "Good morning!"

The two nurses returned the greeting. "How is everything around here?" James asked.

"Quiet." Eddie smiled. "There wasn't a hint of trouble over the weekend."

"Oh, good," Anabelle said. "Hopefully, we can put that behind us."

Eddie agreed and added, "Although I hope we eventually find whoever is responsible. Chances are, whoever it is will strike again if he isn't arrested soon."

Anabelle knew nothing about the pathology of a vandal, and so she simply nodded her head in agreement. Of course, the best thing was for the perpetrator to be caught, but hopefully, in the meantime, the hospital wouldn't be harmed anymore than it already had been.

"Here's hoping for an uneventful day," James said, as Eddie stepped past them.

"Hear, hear," the custodian said, holding the pruning shears above his head. "Take care." He was outside now, smiling at them through the glass.

"Is Gideon's new friend back in town?" Anabelle asked.

"He's coming back this morning," James answered. "I think."

"Oh." Anabelle hoped it was a coincidence that there hadn't been any vandalism while Justin was out of town. If James was thinking the same thing, he wasn't saying anything. They took the elevator to the third floor together. "Have a good day," Anabelle said, ducking into the women's locker room.

"You too," James called out, seemingly lost in thought.

A half hour later, after report, Anabelle stepped into Marcia Barnes's room. "I'm going home today," the woman said. She sat up in the bed and had her hair combed.

"That's great," Anabelle said.

"The social worker got our electricity back on and she got a message through to Dan. He's on his way. And I'm definitely feeling stronger. The new medicine is working."

"Excellent!" Anabelle stepped around the bed where she could read the monitor. Marcia's blood pressure was 128/75 and her pulse was 82. Both vitals were good. "Has Dr. Hildebrand spoken with you about rehab?"

"I think our insurance is at its limit," Marcia said. "And we're already buried in bills."

"Did the social worker look into another plan for you?"

"Yes—but she doesn't have an answer yet."

"It's in their best interest for your insurance company to pay for rehab—it will cost more in the long run if they don't." Anabelle validated the vital signs in the computer and then scanned the notes on Marcia. An order for rehab had already been placed as well as instructions on diet and exercise. A patient who didn't have aftercare was much more likely to suffer a second heart attack than a patient who went through rehabilitation and education. She kept reading Marcia's notes.

"Dr. Hamilton forgot to okay your discharge," Anabelle said. Dr. Hildebrand had attended a conference in Springfield over the weekend and wouldn't be back at the hospital until the next day, so Dr. Hamilton was in charge. "He should be by in the next half hour or so. He does his rounds before his office opens at nine."

Marcia pressed the button on the side railing and the bed moved her into a sitting position. "Dan won't be here for a while anyway. He was going to leave Chicago this morning."

Anabelle would believe it when she met Dan in person.

"I think everyone thinks Dan has abandoned Justin and me," Marcia said.

Anabelle smiled. Could the woman read her mind?

"But he hasn't." Marcia's voice was barely audible. "I promise you he hasn't."

As it turned out, Dan Barnes did in fact exist, though he didn't show up until hours later, not until two thirty that afternoon. The man stood for a moment at the nurses' station looking lost and forlorn. Anabelle spotted him first and asked if she could help him.

"I'm here for Marcia Barnes," he said. "To take her home."

"And you are?" she asked, even though she knew.

"Her husband." His dark hair was peppered with gray, and he wore it long on his neck. "Dan Barnes." His face was lined and weathered as if he spent most of his time outside, and he wore faded levis with holes in the knees, a brown suede jacket, and work boots.

"I'm pleased to meet you. I'm Anabelle Scott, the charge nurse." She extended her hand. He took it quickly and shook it with a grip that was firmer than what she expected.

"Wait a second while I let the social worker know you're here." She didn't want to send him down alone, just in case—

"Social worker?" His brown eyes were puzzled.

Anabelle nodded. "She's arranged some services for your family. She needs to meet with you."

"Oh." He stood completely still, his hands back in his pockets.

Anabelle stepped to the desk and quickly called Janice. "Meet us in Marcia's room, please, ASAP." She hung up the phone and then started down the hall. "Follow me," she said to Dan. He stepped beside her like an obedient puppy. He seemed like a quiet soul, and Anabelle couldn't imagine him striking Marcia, but she knew that abusers came in all types.

She stepped back as they reached the door and Dan slipped in first.

"Baby," he said, "I was so worried about you." He was immediately at the side of the bed, pulling Marcia into his arms. "I'm so sorry I wasn't here for you." He kissed the top of her head as he held her.

Anabelle couldn't see Marcia's face at first, but then Dan sat in the chair beside the bed, clinging to her hand. Marcia's face looked years younger. For the first time since Anabelle met her, the tendons in her neck weren't taut.

"I get to take you home—after we talk with the social worker," Dan said.

"She got the electricity turned back on at the house."

Dan's eyes fell to the floor.

"And she found you."

He nodded but his face wasn't visible. "How's Justin?" His voice was low.

"Out of sorts. He did great that night—probably saved my life. But he's been so worried. He spent the weekend in Princeton with Mother and Dad."

Dan's head jerked up.

"What else could I do?" Marcia's voice was shaky. "He told me he was staying with a friend, but he'd been staying at the house by himself."

Dan shook his head and gripped the side rail of the bed.

"How'd the trip go?" Marcia asked.

"Not so good," he muttered. "No one's looking for a framer right now. I chased rabbit trail after rabbit trail. It's not any better there than it is here."

Marcia stroked his hand but didn't say anything.

"You probably figured out I couldn't pay the cell bill."

"I know," she said.

No wonder Justin couldn't reach his father.

"I didn't mean to stay away so long—I just kept hoping something would turn up. When I found out you were in the hospital, well—"

"*Shh.*" Marcia squeezed his hand.

Anabelle stepped out into the hall, feeling awkward overhearing the couple's personal conversation. Dan was much more likable than she expected him to be. He seemed to genuinely care about Marcia and their son.

Pastor Tom started down the hall toward her, the overhead fluorescent lights bouncing off his silvery brown hair. "Is Marcia still here?"

"Her husband is with her—we're waiting for Janice." Anabelle stepped away from the door and Pastor Tom entered. Anabelle leaned against the wall and looked at her watch. She still needed to finish up the assignments for the next shift. Janice was notoriously late.

She could hear Pastor Tom's soothing voice as he talked with the couple. "Do you mind if I pray?" he asked.

Anabelle couldn't hear Dan and Marcia's response, but a second later, Pastor Tom said, "Dear Lord, we ask for healing for Marcia and that You would meet the financial, emotional, and spiritual needs of this family . . ."

Janice stepped off the elevator as Pastor Tom said, "Amen." She started down the hall, a file and notebook in her hand, and waved to Anabelle when she saw her. Together they walked back into the room. Dan sat on the edge of Marcia's bed, hugging her again. Pastor Tom had a hand on each of them.

"This is Janice, the social worker," Anabelle said.

Dan rose and shook Janice's hand. "Thank you for helping us," he said. "I'm so sorry I wasn't here."

Pastor Tom cleared his throat. "I'll be on my way. Please call me if I can help you in any way." He handed his card to Dan and left the room, patting Anabelle's arm as he went through the door.

"There are a few things we need to address," Janice said. "I still haven't heard if you qualify for the state insurance plan, but I'll let you know."

"Thank you." Dan sounded embarrassed and his head hung low.

"We also need to talk about Marcia's bruises," Janice said.

"Bruises?" Dan turned toward his wife. "Baby, what's going on?"

"I fell," Marcia said. "Twice."

Janice's voice was firm. "They're not consistent with the sort of falls she's described."

"Are you saying someone hit her?" He sat down on the bed again and took his wife's hand. "What happened?"

She shook her head and tears filled her eyes. "I fell, that's all."

Anabelle knew Marcia was lying, but she wasn't so sure about Dan. He seemed sincere. Anabelle sighed. This was Janice's territory, not hers.

No one spoke until Janice finally said, "If you have anything you can add to our investigation please let me know. I've notified Family Services—so far they haven't investigated, but they might still choose to." She handed Dan her card, and he wedged it into the pocket of his jacket along with Pastor Tom's.

Next, Janice took a cheap-looking cell phone from her pocket and handed it to Dan. "This is prepaid, fifty minutes, so use it wisely." Next she gave him a pamphlet about food stamps. He winced.

"It's okay to accept help," Janice said. "The electricity is back on for a month, but the food stamps will help you be able to stretch what money you have."

Dan frowned.

"This is no time for pride," Janice said softly. "Marcia needs to eat healthy food now more than ever, and so does your growing boy."

Dan took the pamphlet and stuffed it in his pocket. A moment later Justin burst into the room.

"Dad!" He flew toward his father. Dan stood, enveloping his son in his arms.

Anabelle swallowed hard as Dan patted Justin's back, as one would a baby, and then pulled his son's hood from his head.

Janice waited a moment and then said, "Justin, we were just talking about your mother's bruises."

"I told you Dad didn't do anything. He wouldn't hurt Mom."

"Ever," Dan said.

"It appears that Marcia may be protecting someone," Janice said and then turned toward Justin. "Have you—"

"You think I hit her?" Justin's voice was hoarse.

"I just want to ask you a few questions since our last discussion was—interrupted."

Justin pulled his hood back onto his head. "I'm not sticking around for this." He turned on his heels and brushed past Anabelle as he tore through the door.

Janice stood completely still, clutching the file to her chest. Marcia cried quietly, and Dan ran his hand through his hair and then said, "May I take my wife home now?"

"Yes," Janice said. "But expect a follow-up to this."

"I'll talk to Justin," Dan said. "He's out of sorts. The last few months have been hard on him—and the last two weeks have been a nightmare, I'm sure."

"Call me if you get any information out of him," Janice said, and then whispered, "Or out of Marcia."

A half hour later, Anabelle wheeled Marcia through the main lobby of the hospital, past the sitting area, the main desk, the potted palms on each side of the double doors, and out the exit. Dan jumped out of an old Toyota station wagon with its taillight taped together with duct tape, rushed around the car, and opened the passenger door.

A minute later he buckled Marcia in the front seat and bent down, kissing her cheek. Anabelle pulled the wheelchair backward and watched as the couple drove away.

Justin was nowhere to be seen.

Chapter Eighteen

*J*AMES SAT AT THE TABLE IN THE FAMILY ROOM with the water, electric, cell phone, and natural gas bills in front of him. He opened the checkbook. The gas bill for March was three hundred seventy dollars. He sighed. There was nothing to be done about that. They had to keep the house warm for Fern.

It used to seem that most of the other nurses at the hospital worked to earn spending money, but he knew that wasn't true now. Candace was the sole support of her family, and now that Cameron was retired, Anabelle's income was essential to their household. He was thankful for his job—that was the bottom line—and grateful that Fern's disability money kept them in the black.

He tried not to think too much about how they would finance college for the boys. Thankfully, Gideon was involved in JROTC. That would certainly help. The boys knew they needed to do everything they could to make college a possibility. Maybe that was what worried him about Justin Barnes—the kid didn't look like he had an inkling of what he wanted for his future.

"James?" Fern sat in her rocking chair, her legs tucked up on the ottoman and covered with a quilt.

"Yes."

Her face was pale. "I posted on my list today." Fern belonged to an online support group for people with MS. "About giving myself the injections."

"I'll do that, sweetheart," he said. "Okay?"

She half nodded and returned to the magazine in her lap. He'd given it to her last week, and she had three more days until her next one. He pulled the yellow sticky pad closer and wrote a note to pick up the injection at the pharmacy. Giving oneself an injection was harder than Fern probably realized, especially when there was no need for her to do it.

She'd been reading more in the last couple of days than she had in the last few months. It seemed the injections were making a difference.

James turned his attention back to the bills. It would be time to help Fern up the stairs to get ready for bed in a few minutes.

"Dad," Nelson was at his elbow. "I need you to sign this permission slip."

James took the piece of paper. It was a Scouting form. "What for?"

"Canoeing down the Culver River. I had it in my backpack from that meeting you missed."

"When is it?" It was a typical Scouting release.

Nelson picked at a scab on his arm. "Two weeks."

James put his pen down. "That's too early. The river's going to be too high. What adults were involved in making this decision?" James shook his head as he read through the release again. The assistant scoutmaster, who had overseen the last couple of meetings, seemed to go along with anything the patrol leaders wanted.

"Dad." Nelson crossed his arms. "It will be fine."

"No." James folded the permission slip. "Tell the troop to wait until May."

Nelson turned toward Fern. "Mom?"

She closed her magazine, holding her place with her finger. "I agree with Dad. It's too early in the spring to go canoeing."

James put the form on the pile of bills. He and Fern had canoed the Culver River years ago, in June. It had been a lovely, beautiful trip.

"We'll be really careful," Nelson said.

James stood and put his hand on Nelson's shoulder. "As scoutmaster, I'll send an e-mail to all of the parents telling them the trip has been postponed."

"Dad—why?"

"The river is high. There's debris floating in it—logs and snags. If a canoe tips, it could be tragic."

"We'll wear life jackets."

"Of course you will." James patted Nelson on the back. "In May. Late May."

"We've already decided," Nelson said.

"Not without permission."

Nelson crossed his arms again.

"Son, it's a closed case." James sat back down.

"What if I'm the only Scout not allowed to go?"

"You won't be," James said. He wasn't so sure that all the other parents would agree with him, but it didn't matter. It was a decision he had to make.

"Would you ask Gideon to come down?" Fern smiled at Nelson as she rocked her chair.

Nelson nodded as he turned toward the stairs.

James wrote a check for the gas bill and recorded it in the registry. He had meant, several times, to put all of their bills online, but hadn't found the time to do it.

Gideon strode into the room. "Nelson said you wanted me."

"How's your homework going?" Fern smiled at their son.

"Fine. I finished my geometry," Gideon said.

"Good." Fern stopped rocking. "And I forgot to ask about Justin and his family. How are they doing?"

Gideon shrugged and glanced at James. "Okay, I guess."

"Was Justin at school today?"

Gideon nodded.

"What did he say?" Fern swung her feet off the ottoman.

"Not much."

"Is he happy his family's back together?" James asked.

"Probably."

Gideon's one-word answers were starting to annoy James, and he aimed to change the subject. "How about inviting Justin to youth group?" James had been thinking it could help give the boy some direction and structure.

"I don't think it's his thing."

"Well, think about it," James said. If Gideon was going to pal around with Justin, at least youth group would be a safe place.

James stirred, stretching out his feet to the end of the mattress. He turned toward Fern and reached for her hand. She was relaxed and still. Something had woken him but it wasn't her. The digital clock read 1:26. He started to drift back to sleep but woke again to what sounded like footsteps on the stairs. Surely one of the boys wasn't up this late. Maybe one of them was sick.

He slipped out of bed and wiggled his feet into his slippers. He made his way to the door and opened it slowly, hoping the squeaky hinge that he needed to oil wouldn't wake Fern.

He padded down the hall and opened Nelson's door. His window shades were open and the streetlamp cast enough light so that James could make out his son in the bed, lying on his stomach with his face toward the wall. James closed the door and padded down the hall to Gideon's room, feeling a little foolish until he opened his oldest son's door and found an empty bed.

James took a deep breath. Maybe Gideon was sick and needed something from the kitchen. He made his way down the staircase quietly, hoping not to wake Fern or Nelson, and through the family room, turning on the lamp beside Fern's chair as he did. Gideon wasn't in the kitchen so James checked the downstairs bathroom. He wasn't there either. He checked the front door; it was unlocked. James opened it and stepped onto the porch into the warm night. A dog ran along the side of the house kitty-corner to the Bells' home but that was the only movement James could make out.

He locked the door and headed upstairs for his cell phone. Before he opened the door to his room, he quickly opened the door to Nelson's. This time his son was kneeling on his bed at the window. He jerked his head around to face James.

"What's going on?" James asked.

"Uh—I'm not sure." Nelson quickly crawled under his covers.

"Where's Gideon?"

"He said it was an emergency."

"What else did he say?"

Nelson pulled the covers up to his chin. "Nothing."

"I'll bet." James yanked the door shut and then tiptoed into his room, grabbed his cell off the dresser, and dialed Gideon's number as he hurried back down the stairs. He didn't answer.

James stood in the middle of the living room and texted, "CALL ME NOW." James guessed Gideon was out with Justin, but if the kid didn't have a cell phone or landline, how had he gotten ahold of Gideon? And why would he lure Gideon out in the middle of the night? James shook his head, trying to make his suspicions—what if they were smoking pot or doing something worse?—disappear.

He checked his phone to see if Gideon had answered his text. Nothing. He would change out of his pajamas and go look for Gideon. As he turned back to the staircase, Fern's voice came down the steps. "James? What's going on?"

She stood at the top, supported by her walker, wearing her cobalt blue robe. Nelson stood behind her.

James started up the stairs, feeling torn between being honest with his wife and protecting her. "Gideon seems to have gone

AWOL," he said, trying not to sound alarmed. "I'm going to go look for him."

"Did you call him?"

James nodded. "He hasn't answered yet."

She took a few steps backward as he reached the landing.

"You should go back to bed," James said, guiding Fern's elbow as she turned around. "I'll just change and be on my way."

"I'm going with you," Nelson said, hurrying to his room.

"No." James's voice was firm. "You're staying here with your mother. If Gideon comes home before I do, you tell him to call me. Immediately."

James felt a rush of adrenaline as he backed the van out of the driveway. Gideon could be anywhere. Downtown at the square. On his way to Justin's house. Vandalizing Hope Haven. Or only a block away. There was no way to tell.

Even though the night was warm, James shivered as he shifted the van into drive and headed toward town. He slowed as he approached the park, peering into the darkness. He decided to stop the van and look on foot. As he slammed the van door shut, his phone jingled in the pocket of his jacket. He yanked it out, nearly fumbling it to the ground. It was Gideon. "Where are you?" James barked.

"Please don't be mad." Gideon sounded terrified.

"Tell me where you are." James tried to soften his voice.

"On the corner of Main and Dill Streets."

"Stay right there," James said. "I'm just a few blocks away." He was already jogging toward the van as he said good-bye.

Gideon stood beside Justin under the streetlamp a block from the town square. His son wore sweatpants and a sweatshirt with the hood pulled tight around his face. He shuffled toward the van as James stopped, but Justin started walking in the opposite direction. James put the van in park. "Justin," he yelled out the open window, "come here."

As Justin shook his head, a police car pulled around the corner.

"Come on." James motioned, and this time Justin obeyed.

As he climbed through the passenger side door of the van, the police car came up along the driver's side. "Hello, James."

It was Cesar, Elena's husband. James stuck his head out the open window.

"What's going on?" Cesar asked.

James nodded his head toward the boys. "My son Gideon and his friend Justin decided to take a little walk."

Cesar climbed from the patrol car. "Is this as far as they got?"

"Boys?" James glanced first at Gideon and then turned his head toward Justin as Cesar shone his flashlight into the van.

"Yes, sir." Gideon's voice was firm. He'd taken off his sweatshirt hood.

"And how about you?" Cesar asked Justin.

"This is my fault. I was upset—Gideon agreed to walk with me."

Cesar hesitated but then turned off the flashlight. "I'll leave them to your care," he said to James.

"Thank you." James exhaled slowly and waited until Cesar climbed into his squad car and drove off. Then he turned to Justin. "I didn't think you had a cell or phone."

He held one up. "My mom got this at the hospital. It's one of those prepaid ones. From that Janice lady." Justin slipped it back into his pocket. It was the most James had heard him say at one time.

"I doubt the social worker intended for you to use it to call Gideon in the middle of the night."

"His parents were arguing," Gideon said. "He needed someone to talk to."

James took a deep breath and exhaled slowly. "So," he said, "you decided to sneak out of the house and scare all of us half to death."

"Mom knows?" Gideon practically whispered.

"Yes. In fact you need to call Nelson and have him tell Mom I found you." James pulled away from the curb as Gideon called his brother.

"You don't have to take me home," Justin said. "I can walk."

"No." James stared straight ahead. "I do have to take you home."

Gideon ended his phone conversation and they rode in silence for a few minutes until James felt as if he might burst. "Look, you both have ill mothers at home who need their rest. This only adds more stress to both our families."

Neither boy responded.

"Plus, when you're out wandering around at night, you're opening yourselves up to being accused of any crime that happens in town." James couldn't stop thinking about the vandalism.

Gideon snorted. "Nothing ever happens around here."

James turned onto the highway. "You'd be surprised."

They rode in silence the rest of the way to Justin's. James turned around in the middle of the street and stopped in front of the house as a man came running out of the house. Marcia appeared in the open door. James didn't say a word as Justin opened his door.

"Get in the house, son," the man said.

James rolled down his window. "I'm Gideon's father—James Bell."

The man didn't offer James his hand but said, "I'm Dan Barnes. Where was he?"

"A few blocks from our house, with Gideon."

"Was there any trouble?" Dan asked, crossing his arms.

"Not that I know of," James answered.

Dan thanked James for bringing his son home, said a quick good night, and headed toward the house.

"I know I messed up," Gideon said as James pulled the van onto the street.

"You're grounded except for church. I'll let you know for how long tomorrow."

"Did you hear about the latest vandalism?" Dr. Hamilton asked James as he washed his hands after the last surgery of the afternoon.

"No." James's stomach fell.

"Another window was broken last night. On the south side of the hospital."

James's heart raced. "Do you know what time?"

"No." Dr. Hamilton turned off the water at the sink he was using. "Why do you ask?"

"Just curious," James answered. *Lord, don't let it be Justin.* He swallowed. *Or Gideon.*

LESLIE GOULD • 180

"Supposedly a story is coming out in today's newspaper." Dr. Hamilton yanked a paper towel from the dispenser.

"Good," James said, turning off his water. "The more people who know about this, the better."

Dr. Hamilton nodded. "See you tomorrow."

After he changed into his street clothes, James ran down the steps to the first floor, out the main entrance, and across the street to the pharmacy. Even in the fresh air, he yawned. He used to be able to survive on a few hours of sleep when he worked night shift back in his twenties, but not anymore. He pushed through the door to the pharmacy and stopped at the end of the "pickup" line. The person ahead of him had a newspaper in her hands. James craned his neck to try to see the front page, but the woman turned slightly and all he could see were the want ads.

The line moved slowly, as each person consulted with the pharmacist. Finally it was his turn. As he approached the counter, he saw a copy of the *Deerford Dispatch* next to the cash register. After he gave the pharmacy tech Fern's name and birthday, he picked up the newspaper while the tech retreated to the back. *Havoc at Hope Haven* read the headline. *By Valera Kincaid*. The story started, *The Hope Haven vandal has struck four times in the last three weeks, including last night around 1:00 AM . . .*

"Here you go." The tech handed him the bag and rang up the order. Without insurance and his Hope Haven discount, the cost would have been nearly five hundred dollars. Thankfully he only had to pay thirty. He handed the tech his debit card and folded the newspaper and returned it to its place by the register.

"Pity, isn't it?" the woman said.

James nodded.

"Sure hope they catch whoever's doing it."

James agreed as he took his receipt and filed it in his wallet to add to the pile of medical expenses at home. He thanked the woman and made his way out of the pharmacy, his heart racing. A light rain fell and James turned up the collar of his jacket. The newspaper would have already been delivered to the house. He stuffed the bag into his jacket pocket and jogged across the street and around to the back of the hospital to the staff parking.

By the number of empty spaces in the parking lot, most of the day-shift staff had left. Relief swept over him as he climbed into the van. He didn't want to talk to anyone. As he pulled out of his parking place, Anabelle waved from the sidewalk, a smile on her face. James nodded and drove on by, grateful he was a few minutes ahead of her. He might have blurted out his fear prematurely.

Ten minutes later, he bolted up the porch to the house and checked the newspaper box. It was empty. Maybe it hadn't come yet. He opened the door quickly and stepped inside.

"James?" It was Fern's sweet voice.

"Be right there." He hung up his coat and walked into the living room.

Fern sat on the couch with Gideon beside her. She held the newspaper in her lap. "Did you see this?" she asked.

James sat on the arm of the couch beside her. "I did. At the pharmacy a few minutes ago."

Gideon groaned. "I swear to you, Dad, Justin and I had nothing to do with vandalizing the hospital. Why would I do that?"

James leaned forward and made eye contact with his son. "Justin could have broken the window before he met you."

"No." Gideon's voice was shrill. "He would never do that. I know he wouldn't."

Elena unlocked the back door of her home and opened it wide, motioning, with a smile, for Izzy to enter first. Her granddaughter's hair was in two long pigtails, and she wore her pink jacket with her purple backpack strapped over it, covering her from the top of her shoulders to the small of her back, giving the appearance of a turtle standing on two legs. A cute, cute turtle.

Izzy kicked off her shoes and then began hopping from black square to black square across Elena's checkered kitchen linoleum. "*Buela*," her granddaughter called out as Elena hung her keys on the peg by the door.

"What, sweetie?"

"Can we pick a bouquet of flowers?"

Elena put her hand to her forehead. She'd planned to roast a chicken and vegetables for dinner, plus she needed to get a load of laundry started.

Izzy reached the last black square of linoleum at the doorway to the dining room, spun around, took a little bow, and then smiled at her grandmother as she shed her backpack. It landed on the floor with a thud. "We could put the flowers on the table for dinner."

"Any special occasion?"

"Just 'cuz."

"'Cuz why?"

"'Cuz I love you, that's why." Izzy came back across the linoleum at a run and Elena kneeled down and spread out her arms. The little girl hugged her tightly and then finally pulled back. "Can we?"

"Of course," Elena said. "Then you can help me get dinner started. Go hang up your backpack and change into your play clothes." Cesar had been working extra hours trying to catch the Hope Haven vandal and Rafael had band practice. If she was a half hour late starting dinner, it wouldn't matter.

As Elena waited for Izzy, she stared out the kitchen window at the pale pink and lavender tulips, swaying in the breeze, trying to imagine what Izzy would be like when she was a young woman. Anabelle had done such a good job with Ainslee and Kirstie. Elena prayed that Izzy would grow up to be as kind and gracious as those girls—and that God would guide Elena in helping to raise her granddaughter.

A robin took off from the grass, a worm in its beak, and flew up into the maple tree. Elena hadn't realized there was a nest so close. She and Izzy would look for it while they cut flowers.

She suddenly felt very aware of the person Izzy was becoming. She didn't remember that awareness as a mother. She was so consumed by each stage of Rafael's childhood that she didn't comprehend that each of those phases was contributing to the man he was to become.

"*Buela*. I can't find my gardening clogs!" Izzy stood in the doorway wearing last year's jeans that hit above her ankles and an old sweatshirt.

"They're right here," Elena said. "By the back door, where they belong."

Izzy giggled and slid across the floor in her stocking feet.

Elena scooped her up and lifted her high, lowering her down into her clogs. Now Izzy was laughing out loud. Elena couldn't help but join her granddaughter. Sure, she wondered who the little girl would become, but she couldn't help but enjoy who she was right now. Being with Izzy was all about being in the moment.

Chapter Nineteen

TUESDAY AFTER WORK, ANABELLE PARKED HER CAR IN the small lot beside the Cavendish House. She didn't see Ainslee's red Honda anywhere. She was sure her daughter still had finishing touches to do on the baby's quilt because Anabelle couldn't imagine that Ainslee would do it on her own outside of the quilting guild. Walking around to the back of the car, she opened the trunk, lifted her plastic box of supplies and fabric, and then started around to the front of the historic house. Pots of greenery accented the porch in front of each of the Corinthian columns.

Anabelle balanced the box on her hip as she unlocked the front door. "Yoo-hoo," she called out. No one answered. The curator was already gone for the day. She made her way up the open staircase along the shiny oak banister to the landing of the mansion, shifted the box to the other hip, and then continued to the second floor. At the end of the long hall was the meeting room where the guild met. Anabelle pushed the door open with her knee.

She opened the drapes at both the side and the back of the room, letting in the spring sunshine and the view of the maple and beech trees that the Cavendish family had planted a hundred and fifty years ago around the perimeter of the grounds. The tender green leaves fluttered in the breeze.

She arranged the tables into a U shape, which provided the best interaction between the quilters. They could all see each other and talk as they worked. She pulled the blue and yellow fabric she purchased in Princeton, her cutting board, roller, and patterns out of her box. She hadn't bothered to bring her sewing machine today. She would concentrate on cutting the squares for the window-seat lap quilt and then do her piecing at home over the weekend.

She heard a car door slam outside and walked to the window. Elena's Jeep was in the lot, and in a second her friend appeared from around the back of it, her sewing machine in one hand and a canvas bag in the other. Elena turned toward something, and Anabelle craned her head to get a better view. Ainslee was coming up behind her, a basket hanging on the crook of her arm. She wore a trench coat, open to the breeze. It was obvious that she couldn't button the coat. She greeted Elena and then reached for her bag. The older woman shook her head and they laughed, but then Elena let Ainslee take it, and she carried her machine with both hands.

Anabelle hurried from the room and down the hall, meeting the women on the landing. She greeted them quickly and then said, "Let me help," and reached for the bag. Ainslee sighed and let her take it, but when Anabelle reached for her daughter's sewing basket, Ainslee told her not to be ridiculous. "I'm fine, Mother," she said, marching ahead, up the stairs.

"She really is fine," Elena whispered. "Look at her—she's doing great."

Anabelle made a face. "I know," she said, her voice falling. Here she'd gotten off on the wrong foot already, and the meeting hadn't even started.

A few minutes later, as Ainslee shed her coat she asked Anabelle, "Where's your machine?"

"I didn't bring it." Anabelle placed Elena's bag on the table adjacent to hers.

"You're kidding." Ainslee crossed her arms over her belly. "How am I going to finish the quilt?"

"I didn't know you needed it," Anabelle said. Ainslee had brought her own machine to the other meetings.

Ainslee exhaled. "Can you go get it?"

Before Anabelle answered, before she even knew what to answer, Elena chimed in. "Use my machine. I have plenty of other stuff to do."

"I'm not good with new machines." Ainslee sank down into a chair.

"Mine's really easy." Elena opened the case of her Bernina. "I promise."

"I always mess up the tension." Ainslee wore the expression of a thirteen-year-old faced with a daunting task.

"I'll help you," Elena said. "I promise."

The other women arrived and began setting up their supplies. Elena readied her machine for Ainslee and then took down her log cabin quilt that had been on display in the room for the last year over one of the blackboards that had been used by the Cavendish children all those years ago, saying it was time for her to take it home and wash it. The quilt was made with shades of orange, reds, and pinks. "Besides," she said, "I think it would look great on Izzy's bed."

Anabelle smiled, thinking of the pink fabric she had tucked away at home just in case Ainslee's baby was a girl. She could see that having a grandchild would increase her motivation to quilt even more, if that were possible.

She laid out her fabric and positioned a pattern.

"What are you making?" Elena asked.

"A quilt for the window seat."

"What about the aprons?" Ainslee scooted closer to the machine, the sage and yellow quilt spread over her bump.

"I decided to wear those," she answered. "You were right—I couldn't bear the thought of cutting them up."

Ainslee smiled, obviously pleased.

Maybe that was what Ainslee needed—to be affirmed in her opinions.

Ainslee hunched over the machine, biting her lower lip, as Genevieve Hamilton, who sat across the room, asked, "Ainslee, when are you due?"

"Two weeks." Ainslee poked her head around her machine. Genevieve asked about her nursery and Ainslee began describing it.

"You must be so excited," Elena said to Anabelle. "I envy you being able to be at the birth." Anabelle took off her reading glasses so she could see Elena better; she must have had a wounded expression on her face.

"What's the matter?" Elena asked.

As Ainslee cleared her throat, Anabelle wished she would have told Elena the day they went to Princeton that Ainslee hadn't made a decision about the subject yet.

"Actually," Ainslee said, "Mother isn't going to be with me during labor and delivery. Doug and I want it to be a private"— she paused—"event."

"Oh." Elena's brown eyes met Anabelle's accompanied by a look of sympathy.

Anabelle's heart sank. There it was. Ainslee had made her decision. She put her reading glasses back on and resumed pinning the pieces of the sample block in front of her, blinking quickly, hoping no one could see the tears filling her eyes.

Chapter Twenty

*D*O YOU WANT ME TO COME WITH YOU?" HEATH ASKED Candace. They stood in the middle of the staff parking lot after their shift ended, discussing the karate program at the Methodist Church. He had to be the sweetest man Candace knew. "No. I'm fine, really. I just appreciate your recommending it."

His gaze was kind and supportive. "Let me know how it goes, okay?"

She nodded. She had his number from when he made birdhouses with the kids. "Thanks," she said. They headed to their cars, and Heath waited until Candace backed out of her space, and then he followed her in his Toyota pickup. She turned right on Whittington Street and then watched in her rearview mirror as Heath turned left, and she wondered if he was going home to an empty house.

She slowed as she neared downtown and then pulled over in front of the church. As she turned off the car, a mother with two boys and a girl wearing white karate uniforms hurried through a side door. Candace followed. The door led to a recreation room with an American flag and a Christian flag on the stage and paneling on the three other walls. The floor was covered with mats and children, around ages five to eight, both boys and girls, all wearing white garb, posed with one foot forward and both arms at their sides. A leader stood at the front, demonstrating a move. He was fairly short with jet black hair and a slim physique.

Candace stood and watched for several minutes as the children imitated the leader. After a while he said, "Okay, that's our warm-up. Who wants to lead the Bible verse for this week?"

Hands shot up all around the room, and he called on a small girl in the middle of the room. Candace recognized her from Howie's class—her name was Madeline, and she had red hair. The little girl wove her way through the other children and stood beside the leader. She smiled and then boomed, "Psalm 119:165. 'Great peace have they who love your law, and nothing can make them stumble.'" When she finished, she smiled again, this time showing her missing two top teeth. Candace wanted to clap but refrained.

"Excellent," the leader said. "Following God's commandments helps us to be able to control ourselves and to do the right thing in every situation." He jumped onto the stage. "It's time now to get together with your partner and practice your foot techniques."

The group milled around.

"Silently and efficiently," the leader called out.

The noise level in the room decreased as the children moved into pairs, swinging their legs back and forth in a choreographed exercise with the child across from them.

The leader was beside Candace before she realized he had left the stage. "I'm Jason Hanson," he said.

Candace introduced herself and told him about Howie and that she was looking for a program with physical activity that promoted discipline.

"That's us," Jason said. "Plus a curriculum that teaches the children to look to God for guidance."

"I like that—a lot," Candace said.

"Why don't you bring Howie by and have him check out the program? He can join us in the drills if he likes." Jason kept his eyes on the kids as he spoke. "In the meantime," he said, glancing back at Candace, "why don't you talk with Madeline's mom? She just started last week and is having a great time. She's the little one who said the verse."

Candace nodded.

"Her mom is over there." He pointed across the room. "Third one from the left."

Candace didn't remember the woman's name but she recognized her. She thanked Jason and made her way around the rec room, circling wide of the children, who were lunging back and forth, their hands in fists, their arms flailing forward and backward.

"Hello," Madeline's mother said as she approached.

"Candace Crenshaw. I'm Howie's mom."

The woman extended her hand. "I'm Sonja."

Candace nodded as she shook the woman's hand. "Jason said that Madeline just started."

"She's an only child." Sonja had curly red hair like her daughter's that she pushed away from her face. "We thought this would be a good chance for her to burn some energy and socialize with other kids."

Candace started to ask more questions but then decided not to. She willed her voice to sound cheery. "So, how does Madeline like karate?"

Sonja shifted her eyes back to Candace. "More than I had even hoped. The activity is great, plus we recite the Bible verses in the car together when we're driving around. We both love it."

"I'm thinking about signing up Howie."

"You should—Madeline would love to have him here."

The two women watched together for a minute. Madeline lunged with a jerk and almost fell over, grabbing onto her partner for support. She laughed and then tried it again. "She's precious," Candace said.

Sonja agreed, and Candace thanked her and said she would see her soon. As she walked to the exit along the back of the room, Jason called for the children's attention and said he had a new move to teach them. By the time she reached the door to the parking lot, the children were completely quiet and only Jason's voice could be heard.

Janet stood in the driveway as Candace approached the house. Howie had a ball in his hands and was only wearing a long-sleeved T-shirt. Her mother wore her long brown coat, gloves, and a hat. As Candace climbed out of her car, she could see that Janet's cheeks were rosy and that her eyes were lit with fun.

Howie slammed the ball to Janet; but she missed it, and he danced around in a circle, shouting, "You're out!"

"Look who's here."

"Mommy!" Howie ran toward her, his hands spinning around like a windmill. "You're home."

Candace stopped on the sidewalk and opened her arms. He rushed into them, nearly knocking her down. She hugged her son tightly. She couldn't imagine her life without her children. They were her inspiration to keep moving forward. She knew, if she didn't have children, God would have provided another incentive, but as it was, Brooke and Howie were more than she needed to keep persevering and to enjoy life in the midst of her ongoing grief.

"How was school?" she asked Howie, taking his hand.

His head bobbed from side to side. "Not too good."

Candace shot a look to her mother and Janet shrugged. "What happened?" Candace asked.

"I had to take a time-out." He hung his head and his voice was low.

"Why?" Candace led the way toward the house as they talked.

"It was time for recess, and I couldn't wait." He looked up at her as if that explained everything. "I ran in the classroom when I was supposed to walk."

That didn't sound so horrible.

"Howie, tell the whole story." Mom was behind them now, the ball in her hand.

"I bumped into someone."

"Who?" Candace asked.

He hung his head. "Mrs. Gray."

For a second Candace wanted to laugh.

"And knocked her down." Howie's voice was barely audible.

"What?" Candace forgot her amusement and tried to keep her voice calm. "Is she all right?"

"She is," Janet said, alongside Candace now. "But she fell against a desk and she hit her elbow pretty hard."

"But Mommy, I said, 'Coming through, coming through,'" Howie added. "I thought she was out of the way."

"Howie." Candace's heart sank as she opened the door.

"He already wrote an apology." Her mother stepped inside first. "It's in his backpack to give to Mrs. Gray."

"I'll call her right now," Candace said.

"Good idea." Janet put the ball in the sports box, and Howie nodded his bare little head, his straight hair flopping up and down.

Candace hurried upstairs to her room, where Howie wouldn't hear, and collapsed on her bed, her coat still on. It was four forty. She hoped Mrs. Gray was still at the school. She dug her cell out of her purse and hit the speed dial for the school. The phone rang and rang but no one answered. She pushed End, stood, and took off her coat as her cell rang. She answered it quickly and said hello.

"Hello. It's Mrs. Gray—"

"How are you?" Candace sat back on the bed.

"Did your mother tell you what happened?"

"Yes."

"When is your appointment with Dr. Lloyd?"

"It was two weeks ago."

There was a pause and then, "You didn't update me. So I'm assuming Howie has started meds."

"No. Actually he hasn't. I haven't decided what to do yet. I'm looking into some other—treatment," she said.

"Well, good luck with that." The tone in Mrs. Gray's voice startled Candace. "All I can say is that I won't tolerate any more behavior like today."

"Yes, I understand," Candace said. After Mrs. Gray hung up, Candace plopped back onto her bed and stared at the ceiling. "God," she whispered. "You said You would be a father to the fatherless. What should I do?" She concentrated on a darker area of the ceiling. She couldn't tell if it was from the later afternoon shadows or if it needed another coat of paint. She closed her eyes. Dean had liked to paint; she hated to.

"Candace." Her mother knocked gently on her door.

She sat up. "Come in," she answered.

The door opened slowly, but before Janet could step into the room, Howie zipped around his grandmother, bounded over to the bed, and climbed onto it. He bounced a little as he plopped down and then turned his head up toward Candace, a big smile on his face. Candace wrapped her arms around him and he hugged her back.

Janet sat down on the other side of him. "Did you think more about getting a second opinion?" She spoke over Howie's head.

Candace still hadn't done it. She was afraid a second opinion might confirm the first. "I still need to call Dr. Amy."

"Why don't you do that now?"

"Now?" Candace glanced at Howie.

"It's the end of her day—maybe she'd be able to talk with you."

Candace bit her lip. The thing with Dr. Amy was, if she could, she would make time to meet with the parent of a patient on the spur of the moment. She had been Howie and Brooke's pediatrician since each was a newborn. She was the kind of doctor who would get down on the floor with a child, and then stand and hug the mother and say kindly, "And how are you doing?" Of course she should call Dr. Amy. Her mother was right.

A half hour later, Candace sat in Dr. Amy's small conference room. The doctor had suggested she come in without Howie. She said she had a handout for parents about ADD and could answer Candace's questions. If necessary, they would schedule an appointment for Howie.

Dr. Amy had dark, shoulder-length hair, pulled back in a tortoiseshell barrette. Her style was simple and her persona serene, even though she had teenage children. The conference room walls were covered with photos of children from around the world—a little boy in Africa playing with a goat, a little girl in Asia riding a water buffalo, an Eskimo child bundled in a fur parka, a boy in Haiti carrying a bag of rice. Dr. Amy had traveled to all of those places on mission trips and had taken all of the photos.

Candace settled back against the back of the chair she sat in, the handout from Dr. Amy in her hand. "I should have called you a couple of weeks ago." She explained what was going on, including the trip to see Dr. Lloyd and both conversations with Mrs. Gray. "I'm not sure what to do. Medication seems so drastic for a kindergartner. I'd like to avoid it if we could."

"Some doctors may be too quick in prescribing medication, but for a small number of young children, medication is the best answer. I tell the parents that they are the experts when it comes to their children. You know Howie better than anyone. We could take a wait-and-see approach over the next several months and reevaluate options then. In the meantime, work on altering Howie's environment. Diet. Exercise—"

"I'm considering signing him up for karate."

"Perfect," Dr. Amy said. "The more activity the better." She raised her eyebrows. "I know you know to limit screen time."

Candace nodded.

Dr. Amy laughed. "And we all know how hard it is. It's a constant struggle at our house."

"What would you do if Howie were your son?" Candace asked.

The doctor chuckled. "Read the handout. I compiled it because I've gone through what you're going through—except with my daughter. She's fifteen now and doing fine, but we had years of turmoil surrounding her ADD."

"Did you put her on meds?"

"Eventually. Like you, it was our very last resort, but it ultimately worked very well for her. In fact, her new doctor is Dr. Lloyd."

Candace absorbed Dr. Amy's words.

They chatted for a few more minutes. When it came time for Candace to leave, Dr. Amy gave her a look of compassion. "I know this is hard. Take it a day at a time—an hour at a time if you need to. But know that there's hope. Things will work out for Howie."

As Candace left the doctor's office, she felt calm for the first time in weeks. Dr. Amy had struggled and come through with the right solution for her family. Somehow Candace would know what was right for hers.

The next day, Candace mulled over both what Mrs. Gray and Dr. Amy had said. Several times she took the prescription from Dr. Lloyd out of her purse and thought about driving over to the hospital and dropping it off at the pharmacy, but then she put it back again. When she realized she was obsessing about her conversation with Mrs. Gray, she would pray about it and try to focus on Dr. Amy's advice. She even reread the handout when she arrived home from work a few minutes earlier than usual. It presented several case histories, including Dr. Amy's experience with her daughter. Unfortunately none of the children's experiences was exactly like Howie's.

Janet sat at the grand piano in the living room, practicing her scales as Candace put on her coat to pick up Howie from school.

"Are you coming right back home?"

Candace shook her head. "I'm going to take Howie by the karate club. I think it's worth a try." Candace grabbed her purse, aware of the prescription inside. "Could you check in with Brooke about her homework?"

"Sure."

"Thank you, Mom." Candace slipped out the door, whispering a prayer of gratitude for her wonderful, accommodating mother.

She met Howie at the side door as school dismissed. Mrs. Gray was deep in conversation with Madeline's mom, which was a relief in that she didn't want to talk with the teacher again so soon, but she had wanted to touch base with Sonja to see if they were going to karate today. She would soon find out.

She waited until Howie was buckled in his booster seat and they were on the road to tell him her plan. "We're going to the Methodist Church. They have a karate class for kids."

"Karate?"

Candace watched in the rearview mirror as he made slashing motions with his hands.

"Madeline does karate. She showed me some moves."

"Really?" Candace pulled out of the parking lot. "Well, that's where we're going, right now."

"Cool!" By the movement in the backseat he continued his killer slashes. "But what about the pajamas? I don't have those."

Candace chuckled. "We'll talk to Mr. Hanson about that. He's the leader. Today we're going to watch, and then we'll talk about it."

They were the first to arrive. Jason greeted them, cinching his black belt around his waist as he approached and then said, "You must be Howie." He knelt down and put out his hand, and Howie took it, shaking it vigorously.

"Pleased to meet you," Jason said. He explained how the program worked and then asked Howie if he'd like to participate.

Howie wrinkled his nose and looked at Candace.

"What is it?" she asked.

He whispered, "I already told you—I don't have the PJs."

Jason laughed. "We'll get you a pair later—no problem."

Other children had arrived and were filling the room. Candace walked to where the parents were watching the day before and sat down. A few minutes later, Sonja sat beside her and the two watched Madeline greet Howie and then stand beside him.

"He's such a nice boy," Sonja said.

Candace felt her face grow warm. Sonja probably wouldn't say that if she knew what happened the day before. Sonja continued, "If Howie decides to do karate, I could give him rides on the days you work. I already have an extra car seat—for play dates and stuff like that."

"Really? Thank you," Candace said, her eyes growing teary. "I was just praying about that on the way over." She breathed deeply. "You know he can be a little active—"

"Well, sure. He's five."

"And"—Candace felt compelled to tell Sonja what happened, especially if she was going to be picking him up sometimes after school—"yesterday he knocked Mrs. Gray over."

"Not really." Sonja wiggled out of her coat as she spoke and then made eye contact with Candace.

"You were there?"

Sonja nodded. "Howie was moving pretty quickly, but he didn't mean to collide with her. She stepped in front of him at the last minute and tripped. Howie didn't do it on purpose. He was just trying to get outside."

"Oh."

"Has she given you the ADD talk?" Sonja's voice was quiet.

Candace nodded.

"That's why we started Madeline here." Sonja pushed her curly red hair away from her face.

"I wondered." Candace paused and then asked, "Did you take her to the doctor?"

"Mrs. Gray said she'd give us the name of a doctor if some sort of activity program didn't work." Sonja crossed her arms. "It's hard to know if Mrs. Gray is overreacting or if the kids have a problem, but my husband said we should wait and see what Madeline's teacher says next year."

As Jason led the kids in the verse of the week, Madeline stepped closer to Howie.

"You know I volunteer in the classroom a lot," Sonja whispered. "Howie is one of Madeline's favorite friends there. He's a great kid. And just so you know, we talked with the principal about all of this. She said this is Mrs. Gray's first year teaching kindergarten. She's always taught third or fourth grade before this."

Candace wanted to laugh. Those were the golden years of elementary school. The kids knew how to cooperate but weren't preadolescent like they were by fifth grade. It was a hard time for Brooke because of Dean's death, but most of her friends had an easy time through those grades.

Sonja continued, "The principal said Mrs. Gray isn't going to teach kindergarten again—she's going back to the older kids."

Candace inhaled slowly. That explained a lot. She watched a few more minutes until the sound of the outside door caught her attention. Heath stood in front of it, scanning the room.

"Excuse me," Candace said to Sonja and grabbed her purse.

By the time she made it to the exit, Heath had spotted her and was smiling. "You didn't call me."

"I'm sorry. I ran out of time," she answered.

"It looks like Howie likes it." Heath nodded toward the kids.

"I think it's going to be a good fit," Candace said. "Thanks so much for the suggestion." Her heart fluttered a little as she spoke. "What are you doing here?"

He held up the laptop case in his hand. "I'm speaking next week to the senior group about native birds. I stopped to see if my presentation will work with their system."

Heath smiled as Howie nearly bumped into Madeline and then caught his balance. "Well," he said, "I'm going to go check in with the pastor."

Candace found herself wanting him to stay a little longer but didn't say anything.

"See you tomorrow," he said.

"Thanks again, Heath," she said.

He turned toward the exit, and then looked back and said, "I expect a full report."

"Nothing less," she answered and then watched him push through the door.

As she sat back down beside Sonja, the woman asked, "Who was that?"

"A friend from work. He's the one who recommended karate for Howie." Candace's face grew warm as she talked.

"*Hmm*," Sonja said. "Sounds like the kind of friend a single mom needs."

Candace's face was flush now. "It's not like that—"

Sonja's eyes lit up. "You should have seen his face when he saw you."

Candace shook her head. She had seen his face—it looked just like it always did. "Oh, look at Madeline," she said. "She's showing Howie how all this works."

Madeline was positioning his arm and then showing him, by example, where to place his feet. Candace appreciated tomboys, probably because—compared to Susan—she'd been considered one. But in retrospect she hadn't been, not really, even though Dean thought she was when they first met because she loved to hike. *Dean*. She'd made this decision about signing Howie up for the karate club without once considering what he would think. She sank back against the chair—not sure if that was a good thing or a bad thing.

Chapter Twenty-One

ANABELLE COULDN'T HELP BUT STARE AT THE plywood covering the hole where the stained-glass window used to be as she left work. Every time she drove by, her heart sank. She turned her head away and then whispered a prayer that the vandal would be arrested soon. She knew Cesar and the other Deerford police officers were doing all they could. It would probably take a careless move on the part of the vandal for the case to be solved.

Her thoughts shifted to Kirstie as she pulled out of the parking lot. She'd been thinking about Ainslee and the baby so much that she hadn't even asked Kirstie how things were going in her classroom. As she turned onto Rishell Street, she decided to stop by the school. The day was over for the children, but Anabelle knew her daughter's dedication. If she didn't have a meeting, she would still be in her room, preparing for the next day.

She parked across the street and hurried into the school. Evan, Ainslee, and Kirstie had all attended the school, and Anabelle had volunteered and gone on field trips every chance she could. It was a blessing to the whole family that Kirstie had gotten a job here. Anabelle teared up a little as she pushed through the front door. In five more years, her grandchild would be a student here, unless Ainslee and Doug moved across town. She and Cameron would be coming to school plays and concerts again, and for grandparents' day. She shivered as she hurried down the hall toward Kirstie's third grade classroom.

Kirstie looked up from her desk. "Mom!"

Anabelle found an opening in the circle of desks and walked toward her daughter, ducking white origami cranes that were hanging from the ceiling, some of them quite low.

Kirstie stood and laughed. "We've been studying Japan."

Anabelle dodged one crane but another one hit her in the forehead. She gently batted it away. "How would you like to come over for dinner tonight?"

"I'd love to." Kirstie leaned against her cluttered desk. "Oh, wait, I have plans with Heather Miller."

"Invite her along."

"Perfect. The last time we hung out, she was pretty negative. Maybe with you and Dad around, we'll have more to talk about than how bummed out she is right now."

Anabelle thought about the steak in the freezer, plus she'd bought some fresh asparagus day before yesterday at the store. That and baked potatoes would do. Then she remembered Heather's culinary school background and she groaned. "Do you think we can pull off a dinner that would meet Heather's expectations?"

"No." Kirstie laughed. "Don't worry about that. I'm just grateful we'll be in a group."

"You could just say no to her." Anabelle searched her daughter's face as she spoke.

"I want to help her out, really I do. I just don't want to be a captive audience to another rant, that's all."

"How about a walk down to the barn?" Cameron suggested as Anabelle cleared the dinner dishes.

"What's down there?" Heather asked.

"Cats." Kirstie's voice was full of annoyance.

Anabelle picked up the salad bowl as Heather rolled her eyes. "I'd better use the restroom first," the young woman said.

"Down the hall. On the right." Anabelle let out a sigh as Heather shuffled away from the table.

"Mom." Kirstie followed Anabelle into the kitchen. "I don't think I can hang around with her anymore."

"*Shh*, honey. She might hear you." Anabelle had no desire to discuss Heather with Kirstie while she was around, even if she was using the bathroom, but her daughter was right. Heather was negative. Plus she'd dominated the conversation during dinner by complaining about the lack of things to do in Deerford, her father's business decisions, and her mother's false optimism. Her tone was full of blame and judgment that, honestly, Anabelle found hard to take too.

"You don't have to spend time with her," she whispered to Kirstie, as she put away the salad dressing.

"I know, but she doesn't really know anyone in town anymore."

Anabelle closed the refrigerator. Kirstie and Heather had known each other since middle school. By high school, Heather was driving a BMW that was a gift from her father and shopping for all of her clothes in Chicago, including buying two hundred–dollar jeans. The girl didn't have many friends, but she didn't seem to want many either. She was one of those kids who couldn't wait to get out of Deerford.

"So are we going or what?" Heather stood in the doorway of the kitchen. She was still dressing to the nines—skinny jeans, a cashmere sweater, Italian boots, and a silk scarf. Her hair was professionally streaked and cut. No wonder the change in her parents' finances had her so upset; it was a major lifestyle change for her.

"You two go ahead and start with Dad," Anabelle said. "I'll just rinse the plates and catch up with you."

Kirstie called for Cameron and the three of them left through the patio door.

Surprisingly, considering she had been studying to be a chef, Heather hadn't said anything negative about dinner. Cameron had grilled steak and asparagus, and they'd had green salad and garlic bread. Maybe it was one of those meals that couldn't be criticized or, hopefully, the girl had some manners. Anabelle rinsed the last plate and quickly loaded all four in the dishwasher. She dried her hands and then followed the others across the backyard as Sarge came bounding toward them. He stopped a few feet away and shook, flinging drops of water in every direction.

Heather put her hands to her face and turned sideways. "Make him stop," she whined.

"Sarge!" Anabelle called, jogging to catch up with the others. He'd probably rolled in the neighbor's pond. Hopefully he hadn't luxuriated in a few cow pies afterward. "Come!"

He lunged toward Heather and then veered away, bounding to Anabelle. She grabbed his collar and pulled him into the yard, talking to him. "So you took a little dip," she said. "Do you think it's that warm?" Actually it was in the midsixties. The tender green leaves of the elm trees around the house glittered in the evening light, and a robin flew up from the yard to her nest in the cherry tree.

Anabelle clipped Sarge's chain to his collar and then hurried to catch up with the others, but they were already in the barn by the time she reached them.

"Back there is the tool room," Cameron said. "I've been refurbishing some rake handles, that sort—"

"Look, kittens!" Heather interrupted, bending down by the box that Cameron had set up for the mama cat and her babies and scooped up a little calico cat that had her eyes half open. "You just said there were cats—not kittens. How old are they?"

"Three weeks," Anabelle said.

"Can I have one?" She sounded like she was in middle school again.

"They're not old enough to be away from their mother yet." Anabelle wanted to remind Heather that they would soon grow into cats, but she bit her lower lip, literally, to keep from speaking out.

"How old do they have to be?"

"Several more weeks." Cameron stepped forward. He frowned and then said, "We really should take Sarge for a walk, don't you think Anabelle?"

She nodded.

"How about if we all go?" Kirstie said.

"No thanks." Heather put the kitten back down. "I've got to go. I need to redo my résumé."

All of them walked toward the house, and while Cameron grabbed Sarge's leash and transferred him to it, Kirstie and Anabelle waved as Heather climbed into her BMW. As she pulled out of the driveway, Anabelle noticed the for-sale sign in the back window.

Kirstie waved, but as soon as Heather turned the corner she said, "She makes me tired."

"She's a little lost right now with all the changes in her life. You're being a good friend to her, and that's what she needs right now," Anabelle said, admitting to herself that she was weary as well.

Cameron joined them, holding Sarge close to his side. The puppy began to bark, and Cameron tugged on his leash. "What is it, boy?" he asked.

In the distance a figure came toward them.

"What in the world? Who could that be?" They didn't see people out here very often.

Anabelle squinted into the distance. It was a young man— Marcia's son to be exact. He carried a drawing pad at his side and seemed lost in thought. "Justin?" she called out.

He startled. "Oh, hi."

"Do you walk this way often?" Cameron asked when he reached them.

Justin blushed. "No. I was just working on some new draw-ings." He quickly held up the pad, and Anabelle caught a quick glance.

He shuffled his feet.

"Shouldn't you be getting home? It's getting kind of late," Anabelle said.

"Yeah. See you, Mrs. Scott," he said with a small wave.

"He seems like a nice kid," Kirstie said.

Anabelle didn't respond. The first page of Justin's sketchbook looked exactly like what a tagger would do.

Chapter Twenty-Two

JAMES GRABBED THE BAG OF POTATOES FROM THE floor of the pantry, swung it onto the counter, dumped several into the sink, and then pulled a paring knife from the block. Fern could use a peeler like a pro, but he'd never mastered that skill.

It had been a hard day at work, beginning with his arrival. The Hope Haven vandal had struck again the night before, and Eddie was power washing the cement wall first thing. At least James could rest assured that Gideon wasn't involved last night—but he couldn't rule out Justin. Just the thought of it made him feel hollow inside.

"So I'm not grounded from church, right?" Gideon asked from the doorway.

"No," James answered.

Gideon grabbed the peeler from the drawer and started helping. He'd been doing quite a bit of that the last few days, which James appreciated, but, still, he wasn't sure what his son's motivation was. Maybe it was to make things easier for James and Fern or maybe it was to make himself look better. "Does church include youth group?"

"Yes." James cut the peeled potato in fourths and dropped it into the water.

"So I can go tonight?"

"Sure. I'll drive you."

"Okay." Gideon rinsed his potato and reached for the paring knife. "I asked Justin if he'd like to go."

"And?"

"And he said he'd like to."

"Meaning I pick him up and take him home and that's the only contact you have with him?" James guided the knife along the potato.

Gideon nodded his head with gusto.

Theoretically, Gideon and Justin could skip out of youth group, but he really didn't think his son would do that, although he never thought Gideon would sneak out of the house either.

"Shall we have garlic mashed potatoes or plain?" James asked.

"Garlic," Gideon answered. "It's what Mom likes." Gideon loitered.

James stopped paring for a moment. "Tell Justin we'll pick him up at seven fifteen."

"Thanks, Dad." Gideon sounded more lighthearted than he had in days, but James still wasn't sure he could trust his son and was nearly certain he couldn't trust Justin. There was no reason denying it.

They continued peeling the potatoes in silence, and then Gideon sliced the last one and James filled the pot with water.

"Put the peels in the compost bucket," James instructed. He checked on the chicken roasting in the oven. They needed a vegetable too. Hopefully there were green beans in the freezer. He never appreciated how effortlessly Fern had put dinner on the table all those years until it became his responsibility. Still, she handled the menu planning and the shopping lists. All he had to do was follow her instructions, but it was still a major chore, day after day, week after week.

A minute later he stepped into the family room to check on Nelson who was doing his homework, and was surprised to find Fern in her rocking chair, beside the fire. "Aren't you tired?" he asked. She almost always took a nap in the late afternoon.

She shook her head.

"What are you reading?" he asked.

She held up a copy of *The Outsiders*. "Nelson is reading it for English."

"So I heard," James said.

"I read it in high school," Fern said. "I just wanted to be able to discuss it with him."

Nelson jerked his head up and groaned. "I need help with math."

Fern held the book up to her face. "Your turn," she said to James, a hint of teasing in her voice.

James sat down next to Nelson. She definitely seemed better. But it was time for her weekly shot—so she could expect an excruciating headache and a wipeout day tomorrow. He cringed. He hated to do that to her.

"Let's take a look," James said, scooting Nelson's algebra book over. He would think about giving Fern her injection later and concentrate on enjoying this normal family time right now. He almost laughed. Sitting around helping with homework and cooking dinner was a blessing.

"Gideon, I'm going up to the porch with you." James put the van into park and turned off the ignition.

Gideon's chin was down and his arms were crossed. "It's not necessary."

"It is." James opened his door. "And that's final." He led the way with Gideon shuffling behind him. The concrete on the walk was broken, the flowerbeds under the windows were sprouting spring weeds, and the wooden steps were practically stripped of paint. The house was obviously a rental that had fallen into disrepair. James knocked on the door a couple of times and when no one answered, he knocked more forcibly.

After a minute, Dan Barnes answered the door wearing jeans, a torn T-shirt, and a baseball cap, his hair curling around it. "Well, hello," he said, seemingly happy to see them. He glanced behind him. "The place is a mess but come on in. I'll get Justin."

James motioned for Gideon to step inside first and then he followed his son. The house wasn't a mess—it was barely furnished. The only item in the living room was a stool sitting on a newspaper with a can of black spray paint on the floor beside it. Shocked, James averted his gaze. The inside of the house had been as poorly cared for as the outside. Paint was chipping off the woodwork and there were water stains on the ceiling. A green plastic bucket was tucked into the far corner of the living room and the wood floor around it was warped.

"Justin!" Dan's voice carried down the hall.

Marcia sat on a folding chair at a card table in the dining room with a plate in front of her. She said hello and then laughed nervously. "Have a seat if you like." She motioned to the two other folding chairs at the table.

"Oh, we didn't mean to interrupt your dinner," James said. "Please, keep eating."

She nodded and took another bite of what looked like beans and rice.

"How are you feeling?" James asked.

She put her fork down. "Much better, thank you."

Dan stepped away from the hallway. "He's on his way." He motioned to the stool. "Justin picked it up at the secondhand store for a buck—and then found the paint alongside the road on his way home last night. He has an easel in his room and has wanted a stool, you know, for his art." There was a hint of pride in Dan's voice as the boys approached.

But as James followed them to the van, he couldn't get the image of the can of spray paint in the middle of Justin Barnes' living room out of his head.

Fifteen minutes later, after he dropped the boys off at the church, James swung by the hospital, hoping a Deerford police officer might be patrolling the parking lot. He slowed as he passed the chapel window. The plywood was still in place and rumor around Hope Haven today was that enough money hadn't been collected to replace it even though a stained-glass artisan in Springfield could finish and deliver the window within a few weeks as long as she was paid. She was incorporating many of the broken pieces into the design.

The van lurched as James drove over a speed bump. He turned toward the wall in the distance across the lot. Eddie had gotten all of the paint off, but now there were two light spots on the concrete. He would have to power wash the entire wall to make it look unaffected. A police cruiser was parked along the curb in front of the ER.

James climbed from the van and headed to the ER entrance but before he reached the door, Cesar and Anabelle stepped out.

"James." Anabelle wore green ER scrubs. Obviously she'd been recruited to help out again. "What are you doing here?"

"I was hoping to find Cesar."

"Looks like I'm a popular guy tonight," he said, his cap in his hand. "Anabelle had something she needed to tell me too." He broke into a grin and then positioned his cap onto his head and took out a pad and pen from his shirt pocket.

James motioned to Anabelle to go first.

"Oh dear," she said. "I know this is going to sound suspicious, but I feel compelled to say something."

"I'll take it for what it's worth," Cesar said.

"Okay." Anabelle turned to James. "And no offense to you or Gideon. I know Justin is a friend of his."

James's face fell.

"Oh dear," Anabelle said again.

"No, go on." James pushed up the sleeves of his sweatshirt. "We may be thinking the same thing."

Anabelle crossed her arms over her scrub top. "The paint the vandal used was traced to us. I bought it for Cameron to redo the handles of his tools."

Cesar nodded. James tried not to look alarmed. He had no idea.

"We saw Justin Barnes not too far from our place last evening, along the lane, walking. We were headed out farther, but he was headed in, toward our barn. I have no evidence that he took the paint—but it seems like it could be a possibility."

James sighed. "I might be able to add to that. I just picked Justin up at his house to go to youth group with Gideon, and there was a can of black spray paint in his living room. His dad said he found it last night along the highway."

Cesar kept writing even after James stopped speaking and then flipped back through his notebook. "Justin Barnes," he said. "I already have his name in my notes. He was on the Hope Haven property a couple of times when the vandal struck."

James nodded. "His mom was a patient here."

"Do you think he has a motivation?" Cesar asked.

"He felt put out—like the nurses were rude to him, that sort of thing," James explained.

"Really?" Anabelle sounded incredulous. "Why didn't someone tell me?"

James shrugged. "I said that's how he felt. You and the other nurses were just doing your jobs."

Anabelle spoke thoughtfully with a tinge of regret in her voice. "We may not have been tuned into the needs of a teenage boy, especially one without another adult to guide him through all of that."

Cesar cleared his throat. "Sounds like I should pay a visit to Justin Barnes."

James rubbed the side of his head. "He should be home around nine fifteen or so. I'm taking him there after youth group." He felt bad bringing Justin to Cesar's attention, but he would feel a lot worse if he hadn't. Besides, having Anabelle suspicious too confirmed his worries.

James sat down on the edge of the bed beside Fern. "I need to leave to pick up the boys," he said, "but I should give you your shot first."

She shook her head.

"I shouldn't?" James was sure she agreed the shot was helping.

She closed *The Outsiders*. "I already did." She looked pleased with herself.

"When?"

"While I was getting ready for bed." She yawned.

"I didn't think you were serious about this." Hadn't they decided the other night that he would give it to her?

She smiled at him. "I don't want you to have to do it—you do too much already."

"Fern," he said, reaching for her hand. "I don't mind, not at all."

"I know. But I was chatting with some people online, and they all said they do their own injections. They talked me through it—told me to ice the skin first—and it wasn't a problem. Well, not really."

"What does that mean?" He squeezed her hand.

Her brown eyes sparkled. "That you do a better job, that's all. But everyone said it takes practice."

James let go of Fern's hand and spread out beside her on top of the comforter, careful not to bump her. The shot was probably already taking effect. "Did you take Motrin before the shot?"

"Four of them," she said.

"Do you want some more shot-giving techniques?"

"Like?"

"Holding the skin while you inject and then putting your hand over it. It helps take the sting out."

"Thanks." She turned her face toward him. "You can coach me through it next week." She wrinkled her nose. "Sorry— but I had to do this one on my own. Otherwise I would have chickened out."

"I understand," James said. He kissed her lips. "Sweet dreams," he said. By the time he returned he hoped she would be fast asleep.

Fifteen minutes later he waited across the street from Church of the Good Shepherd, drumming his fingers on the steering wheel to the classic rock station. He yawned. How he wished he were still cuddling with Fern. He opened the window and a rush of cool air swept over him. He stuck his head out and turned his face upward. Stars studded the sky and a hint of daphne greeted him, probably from the yard he parked in front of. Fern liked daphne, and he had meant for a couple of years to buy her a bush. Her mom had a plant beside the front door at their place, and it was a pleasant scent to greet people as they arrived or left the house.

James yawned again and pulled his head back into the van. Every time he thought about Justin he felt anxious. "Lord, You know," he whispered. "I don't—so I leave it up to You." He felt a measure of peace for a moment but was jarred out of it as the boys reached the van and yanked open their doors.

"How was it?" James asked, starting the car.

"The music was better than I thought it would be. The sermon was good, too. It was about taking stuff a step at a time."

James exhaled, wondering how Justin would handle this next step coming up in his life. He turned on the headlights and pulled away from the curb. "How many kids were there?" he asked in an effort to make small talk.

"Around thirty," Gideon answered. "The usual."

"There were a lot of kids from school." Justin was silent for a minute. "I'm really bummed we might end up moving to Princeton."

"Why's that?" James asked. He hoped he was disguising his relief. Having Justin move to Princeton would definitely ease his worries.

"We'll live with my grandparents—save on rent."

James realized, by the lack of reaction from his son, that Gideon and Justin must have already discussed the possibility of the move. "There's a good church there—a sister church to ours," James said.

"That's cool." Justin's voice sounded far away. "'Cuz my grandparents' church is a real drag. They used to make me go when I was little."

They rode in silence for a few minutes. As they neared the highway, just a couple of blocks from Hope Haven, James wondered if Cesar would be at Justin's house when they arrived. He hoped not. He stopped at the intersection of Smith Street and Oak Avenue.

"Hey, look." Gideon pointed down the street.

James squinted. Someone dressed in dark clothing and wearing a stocking cap ran down the sidewalk toward them and then darted into a yard.

"Call 911." James tossed his phone at Gideon as he pulled over and put the car in park. Suddenly, he felt a surge of adrenaline reminiscent of his days in the Gulf War. He flung the door open and took off running. His plan was to cut in at the alley and see if he could spot the person. As he hit his stride, he regretted giving Gideon his cell phone and then wondered if it had been wise to leave the van—with the key still in it—at Justin's disposal.

He bounded around a tricycle left on the sidewalk and pushed himself faster, turning into the alley. He stopped for a moment, giving his eyes time to adjust. There was a rustling in the distance. The person came scrambling down the alley toward James just as a police cruiser, its lights flashing, appeared at the other end. James stepped out of the shadows, but the person didn't see him. The figure was slim, and if James didn't know Justin was in the car with Gideon he would think it was him.

"Halt!" James called out, lunging, executing a tackle like he hadn't since high school.

He could feel the air go out of the person, followed by a gasp and then, "Get off me." It was the voice of a girl.

Alarmed, James jumped to his feet. A young woman, flat on her back, scowled at him, holding her arm. "I think you broke it," she said, perfectly illuminated by the flashing lights of the cruiser that were practically on top of them now and by the headlights of the van, that Gideon was inching down the alleyway. She wore jeans and a black sweatshirt.

Cesar jumped from the cruiser and pulled his gun. "Identify yourself."

The girl turned toward him and gave him a dirty look. James stepped backward.

"I said identify yourself!"

She sat up. "Heather Miller." She pulled the stocking cap off her head and blonde hair spilled around her shoulders.

James wanted to gasp. Loren and Leanne's daughter. Her father had been on the board at the hospital. Leanne was a sweet, sweet lady.

"And what business did you have at Hope Haven tonight?" Cesar barked.

"I wasn't at Hope Haven. I was walking home when this guy tackled me." Heather struggled to her feet and James stepped forward and helped her, feeling horrible. "Besides," she said, "I need to talk to my lawyer before I answer any more questions."

"I don't think her arm's broken." Anabelle stood in the hallway with James. "Just bruised. And her parents are here."

"With their lawyer?" James felt the weight of the world on his shoulders.

"James." Cesar stuck his head out of the curtain of the cubicle. "Could you come here?"

He glanced at Gideon and Justin who stood stoically at the end of the hall. "I'll be right back," he said and shuffled down the hall, pushing back the curtain. Anabelle followed him.

Cesar stood at the end of the bed, a video camera in his hands. "Heather has just made a full confession."

She looked smaller in the light of the ER, and even more out of sorts with dirty paths of mascara and tears streaking her cheeks and the sleeve of her sweatshirt cut at a jagged angle. "I didn't mean to do it." The tears started again. "I had a friend in college who used to do some tagging. When I couldn't even get a job in the cafeteria, after all the money dad gave, I decided to tag it. That was all. It's not that big a deal."

"Heather." Her mother sat on the edge of her bed.

"And then I broke a couple of windows."

"Heather," her mother said, stroking her forehead.

James ducked into the hall. Every family had their problems, that was for sure. In a second Anabelle was beside him. "You okay?"

"I feel really bad that I hurt her arm." He ran his hand through his hair as Cesar stepped from the cubicle too.

"I feel bad that you didn't stop to consider she might have a weapon before you tackled her," Cesar said.

Anabelle gasped, but James just shook his head. It hadn't entered his mind that he might be putting himself in danger or that a police officer might already be shadowing the suspect. But Cesar was right. He had Fern and the boys to consider—he couldn't be jumping criminals in alleys. "I need to get Justin home." He shook Cesar's hand and Anabelle followed him down the hall.

"I feel bad that I suspected Justin," she whispered.

"Me too." James hugged Anabelle quickly. "See you later."

"Tell Fern I'll pick her up tomorrow, around seven for Ainslee's shower."

"Oh." He bumped his forehead with the heel of his hand. He still needed to pick up a gift. He hoped Fern would feel up to going to the shower.

As he motioned the boys to follow him, he spotted Loren Miller in the waiting room, his head in his hands. Pastor Tom was sitting next to him.

"Let's get you home," James said to Justin. "I hope your parents aren't frantic." He sighed. "I know I would be. If they're up, I need to explain some things to them."

No one spoke as James turned onto the highway and then onto Justin's street a few moments later. James felt convicted for the things he thought about Justin and his family. As he parked the van, he prayed the Lord would give him the right words as he explained himself to Dan and Marcia Barnes.

They were still up, sitting at the card table. James stood on the porch and watched the couple through the thin window curtain as Dan bounded to his feet at the sound of the front door opening. "Son," he called out. "Is that you?"

James asked if he could join Marcia and Dan at the table and explained what happened as the boys disappeared down the hall to Justin's room.

As James finished detailing the events of the evening, he asked Dan and Marcia to forgive him.

"Whatever for?" Marcia asked.

"I thought the worst of your family," he said, and then admitted that he thought Justin was the vandal.

Dan tipped his chair back and seemed offended but Marcia said, "I understand why you would think that." She took Dan's hand and pulled him back to the table. "We didn't present ourselves very well, and I was evasive—dishonest—about the bruises." She took a sip of coffee. "I called the social worker this morning and 'fessed up though."

Dan squeezed her hand.

"My dad has Alzheimer's," she said.

James nodded. He remembered that.

"I went to ask them for help, right after Dan went to Chicago to look for work. My father got upset, said Dan wasn't taking care of his family. He was very confused and out of sorts. He pushed me then grabbed my arm and yanked me up." She went on to say she didn't want anyone to know at first because she didn't want to cause problems for her parents.

"Has your father been aggressive toward your mother?" James asked.

Marcia nodded. "I called Janice and she gave us some resources in Princeton. We have an appointment with Dad's doctor tomorrow, and then we'll figure out the next step."

She glanced at Dan. "But it looks like we're moving in with them."

Dan nodded, his face grim.

"That's what Justin said." James put his hands down flat on the table. He needed to get going.

"I'll get Gideon," Dan said, standing.

James thanked Marcia for sharing with him. He stood, feeling much lighter.

As he followed Gideon out the door, Dan asked if he could talk to James for a minute.

"Go on out to the car, Gideon. I'll be right there," James said.

The two stood for a moment on the porch, watching Gideon climb into the van. Dan plucked his cap off his head and then repositioned it, backward, yanking it tight. "We had our own place in Chicago. Fixed it up real nice." He inhaled and then let his breath out slowly. "For some reason I thought the boom would last forever, that I would always have work, be a foreman well into my sixties." He toed a chunk of peeling paint. "But then we lost everything." He tried to smile.

James nodded. He couldn't imagine what that would be like.

"Anyway, I just wanted to tell you that. I just wanted you to know that I love my wife. That I love my kid. That I would do anything for them."

James reached out and shook Dan's hand. "I can tell that," he said. "We're all in this life together, just trying to make it through."

Dan Barnes was a good man raising a good son. James was sorry to see them go.

As they pulled away from the curb, Gideon cleared his throat. "Dad." He paused, looking straight ahead. "I'm sorry about sneaking out and getting caught up in Justin's stuff."

"Son, it was okay to want to help Justin." James reached over and patted Gideon's knee. It was the hard times that made a person appreciate what they had. He breathed a prayer that the difficulties in their family, Fern's illness in particular, would make them all closer in the long run.

Chapter Twenty-Three

NABELLE STOPPED HER GROCERY CART IN THE produce section of Deerford Grocery, stifling another yawn. She wasn't going to take any more ER shifts. It was too much. She picked out four gala apples and slipped them into a brown paper bag and then pushed the cart toward the grapes, selecting a small bunch. Shopping for two was much different than shopping for five. It was still difficult for her to get used to buying smaller amounts.

"Anabelle?" Leanne Miller was on the other side of the oranges. "Is that you?"

"It's me." Anabelle pushed her cart around the corner. "How are you holding up?"

Leanne's hair and makeup were perfectly done, and she was dressed in a pantsuit and wearing heels. No one would guess at the stress she was enduring. "Oh, I'm all right. Heather's out on bail. Loren paid it."

"I'm so sorry about all of this." Anabelle gripped the plastic handle of the cart.

"Don't be. It's actually for the best. I think this will be a real turning point for Heather. I have an appointment on Monday with the counselor Heather saw a few years ago. I'm going to insist that she go back."

"That's wise."

"And Pastor Tom came by this morning. Heather asked him to forgive her."

"Well, that's certainly a good place to start," Anabelle said. She wouldn't have expected that from Heather, but perhaps Heather needed to hit rock bottom first before she could prioritize her life.

"Loren and I have paid to replace the stained-glass window, and Heather will pay us back if it takes her fifty years."

A wave of relief swept over Anabelle.

Leanne turned her cart toward the front of the store. "Anyway, I'd better get home." The woman held her head high as she made her way toward the first checkout station. Anabelle imagined how difficult it must be for Leanne to face those who knew what her daughter did. She was reminded of the woman in Proverbs 31, who "clothed herself in strength and dignity." That was Leanne Miller to a T. She wasn't blaming herself for Heather's behavior, and she was thankful that her daughter was getting the help she needed.

Strength and dignity. If only Anabelle could clothe herself in those two values as she faced her own small hurdles. Like the shower tonight. She stood taller. To be honest, she was dreading it. "Strength and dignity," she prayed. "Lord, show me how to live that way."

Anabelle pulled into the Bells' driveway. The heavy front door to the Bell home opened, and James waved. Anabelle hurried around to the passenger side and opened the door. She chastised herself again as she watched Fern come down the cement stairs, one at a time, clutching James's arm. Her problems were minor compared to others'. She needed to stop getting so absorbed in the details of her own life.

"Fern," she said, "you look lovely."

Her friend wore a pleated navy blue skirt and a yellow silk blouse, along with a small beaded purse on a thin strap over her shoulder. Her pixie cut was pulled back on one side with a clip, and her brown eyes shone brightly.

"Thank you," she said, taking another slow step. When she reached the car, she patted James's arm. "Would you please get my walker. I don't think my cane will be enough tonight."

"Will do," James said and hurried back to the house returning a minute later with the folded walker in his hand, carrying it with ease.

Anabelle popped the trunk, and he opened it, slipping the walker inside, and then came around to the side to kiss Fern. "Don't stay out too late," he said.

"We won't," Anabelle assured him. She was tired and besides, she was determined not to hover tonight, not to outstay her welcome, or crowd Ainslee in any way. Having to get Fern home would help her stick to what she had resolved.

"How has your week been?" Anabelle pulled away from the curb.

"Good." Fern sat with her purse in her lap. "Well, it was a little stressful but better now although I had my injection last night and have a headache—but that's better too."

Fern turned toward Anabelle. "How are you? The grandmother-to-be."

Anabelle turned onto Fourth Avenue. "Good." She sat up straight. *Strength and dignity.* If Fern could manage daily life like she did, Anabelle could face this shower with joy. If the subject of the delivery came up she would smile and defer to Ainslee and then keep smiling.

After parking in the driveway and helping Fern into the house and getting her settled, Anabelle brought in their gifts and sat down next to Kirstie and Candace in Elena's living room. They made small chitchat as more and more guests arrived carrying beautifully wrapped gifts.

Anabelle joined Elena at the dining room table as Elena arranged a bouquet of pale yellow tulips. The vase was hidden in a boxy centerpiece made of heavyweight sage paper with an illustration of an old-fashioned pram printed on each side. It was the same design that had been on the handmade invitations. At the end of the table were favor boxes of the same design but on a much smaller scale.

"Elena, this is all so adorable," Anabelle said, stepping closer. She knew her friend was creative—she demonstrated it with every quilt she made—but Anabelle had no idea Elena was this clever. "Where did you come up with these wonderful ideas?"

"Oh," she said, matter-of-factly, "a nice clerk at the craft store gave me a couple of ideas and I ran with them." She positioned the flowers in the middle of the table, on top of a lace overlay. Crystal plates and goblets were arranged in a fan shape. Elena stepped back. "Do you think Ainslee will like it?"

"She'll love it," Anabelle answered. It was as if Ainslee had designed it all herself. "We can't thank you enough for your thoughtfulness, Elena."

Elena smiled and before she could respond, the doorbell rang, and she hurried to the entryway, followed by Anabelle. "Our mother-to-be has arrived!" Elena gave Ainslee a hug and then turned to the group of ladies.

Ainslee held up her hand in a halfhearted wave and then straightened her teal top over her maternity capris. Her face was flush and her hair, which was piled on her head, hung a little more loosely than usual, with wisps hanging alongside her long neck, one entwined in a gold hoop earring.

Elena directed her to the wingback chair to the side of the fireplace, beside the gifts piled on the hearth, and motioned to Anabelle to come sit in the chair beside her daughter. Then the hostess had everyone go around the room and introduce themselves. Most everyone knew each other, or at least knew of each other.

"Now," Elena said. "We're going to play a game." Anabelle braced herself for Ainslee's reaction to parenting advice, but as Elena continued it was obvious she had chosen a different game. "I'm going to ask a series of questions and we're all going to answer them, including Ainslee. Then we'll compare answers." Elena's eyes danced. "Then after we have dessert, we'll play the same game but Anabelle will be in the hot seat."

Anabelle groaned, wondering why she'd agreed to be included in the shower.

The questions for Ainslee were pretty routine. "Do you think the baby is a boy or a girl? How much do you think the baby will weigh? What names do Ainslee and Doug have picked out?" Anabelle left that answer blank. In true Ainslee fashion, she hadn't breathed a word about names. "Does the baby have a bassinet? What percentage of diapers will Ainslee change compared to Doug?" Anabelle stole a look at her daughter, suppressed a laugh, and then returned her attention to the survey. "When will Ainslee leave the baby with a sitter for the first time?" Anabelle decided to leave that one blank too. "What is Ainslee's biggest fear about being a mother?" Anabelle accidentally dropped the pen, sending it scurrying across the floor. "Oops," she said, dashing after it. As she picked it up, she caught another glimpse of Ainslee's face. It looked like she was grimacing—maybe she didn't like the questions either.

After a few more minutes, Elena clapped her hands together and said it was time to put down their pens.

It turned out that Ainslee, and just about everyone in the room, guessed the baby was a girl. "Everyone tells me I'm carrying high," she said, and then blushed. "And I've had a lot of heartburn." She looked from Anabelle to Candace as she spoke but neither said a word.

A few minutes later, after the women had shared what they thought Ainslee would name the baby—Emily, Ashley, Lily, Jessica—Ainslee said, "I've only talked to Doug about names— no one else."

"But do you have an idea?" Candace asked. "You're not going to call her 'Baby' for a year are you?"

Ainslee paused for a moment and shifted in the chair. "Oh heavens, no," she finally said and patted the top of her belly.

Anabelle nearly laughed out loud. All of Ainslee's dolls and stuffed animals had full names—first, middle, and last—when she was little. And histories. She couldn't imagine Ainslee going a minute without naming the baby.

Elena zipped through the questions, and Ainslee gave her answers quickly, smiling and laughing some, but it seemed her mind quickly switched somewhere else. Anabelle watched her daughter with concern but then Elena called for the women's attention again. It was time for dessert, and Elena asked the women to gather in the dining room.

Anabelle stood and knelt down in front of her. "Sweetie," she whispered, "are you okay?"

Ainslee nodded. "I've had indigestion all afternoon plus Braxton Hicks."

Anabelle shot a look at Candace who tapped her watch.

"Nod to me when you feel another one," Anabelle said.

"Okay." Ainslee stayed put in the chair but took a plate of strawberry shortcake from Elena. Anabelle thought that was a good sign, but her daughter just picked at the fruit and then put the plate between two gifts on the mantel, as she nodded to Anabelle.

Anabelle focused on her watch until Ainslee said, "It stopped."

"Fifty seconds," Anabelle said.

"I really don't think it's anything," Ainslee said.

"What's anything?" Kirstie handed Fern a plate of dessert and then sat down beside her.

"None of your beeswax," Ainslee barked.

"Ains," Anabelle whispered.

Kirstie rolled her eyes and muttered, "A pregnant big sister. My worst nightmare."

Candace brought Anabelle a piece of shortcake and then whispered, "How is it going?"

Ainslee gasped, "Oh."

Anabelle held her watch up.

Every woman in the room froze. Forks stopped in midair. Mouths hung half open in midbite. No one spoke. All eyes were on Ainslee as she breathed through the contraction.

Anabelle announced, "Sixty-two seconds."

"Ainslee, you should get going," Candace said. "Your mom needs to take you to the hospital. Call Doug on the way."

"Do I really need to go to the hospital for Braxton Hicks?"

"No," Candace said gently. "You need to go to the hospital because you're in labor."

Ainslee's eyes widened. "But my due date's not for another week!" She looked around the room wild-eyed then back at Candace. A hint of panic tinged her voice. "Will you come too?"

Anabelle's heart fell for a moment. Candace would see her grandchild born, but she wouldn't.

"I'll go if you want me to," Candace said.

Ainslee nodded.

"I'll take Fern home," Kirstie said.

"Elena," Candace said. The hostess stood under the archway between the dining room and living room. "There has been a slight change of plans." Candace smiled. "Instead of a shower—there's going to be a baby."

All of the women began to clap, led by Minnie, who hollered, "I've never been to a shower where the mother-to-be went into labor!" The women cheered. As Ainslee stood, they gathered around her and escorted her out the door, leaving the unopened gifts behind.

Chapter Twenty-Four

ANABELLE SAT IN THE WAITING ROOM OUTSIDE the maternity ward of Hope Haven, hoping Candace was right, praying her grandchild would arrive tonight and not the next day.

She checked her watch again. Cameron should have arrived by now. And she hadn't told Kirstie to come by the hospital after she dropped off Fern, but she had assumed she would.

When Doug had hurried by a half hour ago, he had stopped to hug her. "I'll keep you updated," he called out before he disappeared through the double doors.

It wasn't often that Anabelle was a family member at Hope Haven. In fact she hadn't been since that horrible day when Kirstie was struck by a car and lost her leg. She shivered at the thought and leaned back against the vinyl seat. She was tempted to go down to the CCU and chat with whoever was at the nurses' station to distract herself but quickly decided against it.

What if Ainslee changed her mind and wanted Anabelle to be with her? She sank farther down into the chair. That wasn't going to happen, but she would stay put. She wasn't going to risk being away if she was needed.

Ten minutes later Cameron, followed by Evan and Kirstie, hurried into the waiting room, smiles plastered on their faces. Cameron had two bottles of sparkling cider in his hands and a stack of plastic cups.

"We're not celebrating yet," Anabelle said.

"We will be soon!" Cameron planted a kiss on her cheek, put the cider and glasses on the table, and sat beside Anabelle.

The kids greeted her too, and then Evan said he hadn't had dinner and asked Kirstie if she wanted to go to the cafeteria with him.

"Do we have time?" she asked Anabelle.

"Plenty of time," Anabelle answered, remembering her first labor that went on for over thirty hours.

Cameron took her hand as Evan and Kirstie headed for the elevator.

A few minutes later, Dr. Carpenter bounded off the elevator. "Anabelle!" She greeted them with a smile. "And Cameron. So nice to see you. Looks like tonight is the night."

"Hopefully," Anabelle answered. "Are you here for Ainslee already?"

"I have three moms in labor." Dr. Carpenter pulled her unruly curls back into a ponytail as she spoke. She wore jeans and a sweatshirt. "I came straight from my son's T-ball game—they won." She beamed. "Anyway, Ainslee was the last to come in—so I'm assuming she's not as far along, but I'll soon know for sure." She began walking toward the double doors as she spoke. "Are you coming?" she asked.

Cameron shook his head.

The doctor laughed. "I meant Anabelle."

"No."

The doctor cocked her head. "Well, I'm sure I'll be seeing you soon." She waved and pushed through the doors.

Cameron took Anabelle's hand. "Keep your chin up," he said. "Remember, this is all about the baby—about our grandchild."

She nodded. She knew that. She felt mostly fine—at least she had accepted not being there when the baby was born, until someone brought it up. Then she felt awful again.

A woman, who looked about Ainslee's age and wore a hospital gown and a robe, shuffled through the door, followed by her husband. The woman had one hand resting on her belly and the other on the small of her back. Her husband pushed his glasses up on his nose as he walked beside her, his head bent down to hear her speak.

"It really does feel better to walk," she said. "And the nurse said it might speed labor."

Anabelle tried not to stare as an older woman followed them, probably the woman's mother. "Honey," she said, "are you sure you should be away from your room?"

Anabelle stifled a smile as the young woman gave her mother a look to rival that of a thirteen-year-old, but then she realized she hadn't even talked with Ainslee about what to do in labor.

She sighed. Well, now she had Candace for that, who would be able to give her better advice anyway.

The trio moved on down the hall toward the med floor, and a minute later Hap Winston came by pushing a broom. "Anabelle," he said, leaning against the handle, his voice full of joy. "Is it time?"

"I think so, Hap." She couldn't help but smile.

"Oh, wonderful!" He stepped closer. "You know, this is my favorite floor to work on. I think about those babies and their families and pray up a storm while I work."

Anabelle leaned against Cameron, and he squeezed her hand.

"I'll be saying special prayers for Ainslee all night." He smiled again and pushed the broom forward, a lilt in his step. It was as if he was dancing as he prayed.

"Cameron," Anabelle whispered as Hap rounded the corner. "We should pray." Here she'd been fighting jealousy and resentment all these weeks. Sure, she'd been praying that Ainslee and the baby would be healthy, but at the same time she was focusing on being slighted. She chided herself. *Stop being offended that Ainslee doesn't want you at the birth, and start enjoying every moment possible of this grand adventure.*

Cameron put his arm around her. "Dear Lord, we ask You to protect our daughter Ainslee, to give Doug the strength he needs, and to bring this new babe into the world, healthy and ready to live. And we dedicate the wee one to You." Cameron squeezed her shoulder.

"And thank You for our family and this new addition and for all the ways You have blessed us."

"Amen," Cameron said. They opened their eyes in unison and Cameron leaned forward and kissed her on the lips. "Well, Granny." He grinned. "What a day for us." He kissed her again as Evan and Kirstie appeared.

"*Ahh,*" Kirstie said, "look at the old people." She plopped down across from them and Evan sat beside her, a red and white checked take-out box in his hand.

"I didn't think grandparents did that sort of thing." Evan pointed a french fry at them as he talked.

Cameron hugged Anabelle tighter. "Ah, she'll always be my lassie," he said in an exaggerated Scottish brogue.

Kirstie started to smile but it morphed into a yawn.

"So what's the word?" Evan balanced the box on his lap.

"We haven't heard a thing," Anabelle said.

"That's so unlike Ainslee not to update us." Kirstie sat up straight.

They chatted for a few minutes and then Evan and Kirstie both pulled out their phones. First it appeared they were sending texts, then it seemed they were playing games. The pregnant woman who had walked by earlier, her husband, and her mother all shuffled through the waiting room after a while and back through the doors to the maternity unit.

Anabelle wished she had her sewing basket with her or some yarn and knitting needles. She couldn't stand to sit still any longer and walked around the waiting room until she found a year-old magazine on the corner table and leafed through it. Cameron leaned back and closed his eyes. It was getting close to his bedtime.

They all leaped to their feet when Candace, wearing scrubs, appeared at ten thirty. She motioned for them to sit down. "I just wanted to update you. She's doing great, progressing nicely."

"It could still be a whole lot longer," Anabelle said, putting down the magazine, after Candace returned to the ward.

"Or maybe not," Kirstie said. "A friend of mine from college had a baby last year—it went really quickly."

Anabelle wrinkled her nose. She didn't want to get her hopes up. A minute later Hap came traipsing down the hall, whistling as he walked toward them. "Any news?" he called out.

"She's doing great!" she said. Anabelle knew he had grandchildren, probably even great-grandchildren. She smiled at the thought.

"I'll keep praying." He grinned as he turned the corner toward the elevator.

At eleven Evan said he thought he would go home.

"You can't." Kirstie scowled at her brother.

"It could be hours still," he said, standing.

"It won't be hours. You know Ainslee—she'll have the baby by midnight." Kirstie grabbed the sleeve of his shirt and pulled him back down. "You have to stay."

Evan pushed at Kirstie playfully. "For another half hour— that's it. Someone needs to relay a message to Ainslee that she better get a move on."

The mother of the woman who had been walking earlier came through the doors, clutching her purse, and sat down a few seats away.

"How's it going?" Anabelle asked.

"Good. The doctor said the baby will come soon." The woman took a deep breath. "Do you know where the cafeteria is? I need a cup of coffee—and a break." She shook her head, chuckling.

"First floor," Anabelle said.

The woman thanked her and headed toward the elevator. A couple of minutes later the elevator dinged again and Doug's parents arrived. Louise Giffen rushed off first, and looked side to side for a face she recognized. She was wearing a sapphire sweater and floral scarf around her neck, and clutched her purse tightly. Her husband, George, followed her, shaking his head in amusement at his wife's eagerness.

"It's happening!" Louise said as she approached the group. She and George pushed chairs into the cluster the Scotts had formed. "When Doug called, we had to get here as soon as we could. Even though it's not our first grandchild, we are so excited. This never gets old."

Anabelle nodded. The couple's younger son who lived in Baltimore already had children.

A moment later, Candace swung through the doors, and all six of them stood. "Has the baby come?" Anabelle asked, hoping that's what Candace came to tell them, praying it wasn't bad news.

"No. But everything's fine. She's ready to push." Candace grinned. "And she wants you with her."

Anabelle looked around their small group. Who was Candace speaking to? Doug's mom?

"She wants you, Mother," Kirstie said. "Who else would she want?"

"Me?" Anabelle placed her hand across her chest.

Candace nodded.

"Are you sure?" she whispered.

"Positive." Candace turned on her heels. "Come on though—she says she's going to have this baby ASAP."

Anabelle glanced at Cameron. "Go," he said beaming. "And then come back and tell us the good news."

Anabelle peeked into Ainslee's room and saw her daughter's strained face as Doug held her hand offering encouragement. She didn't like seeing Ainslee in so much pain, but she marveled at her daughter's strength. Candace put her arm around her shoulder. "Can you believe it?" Candace asked.

"She's so strong," Anabelle said, as much to herself as to Candace. And—what was it that she'd been chanting to herself earlier in the evening? *Strength . . . and . . . dignity.* That was it. Now it was her prayer for both her and Ainslee.

"I can do this," she said to Candace, taking a deep breath.

Her friend smiled as she led the way into the birthing suite. "Come on, Grandma."

Through her delirium and strained breathing, Ainslee's expression registered relief when she saw who entered the room. "Mother!"

"You're doing wonderfully, Ains!"

She groaned out a thank-you.

All of Anabelle's attention focused on her daughter. On the third push, as Ainslee squeezed Anabelle's hand, digging her fingernails into her mother's palm as she leaned forward, concentrating with all her might, Dr. Carpenter said, "You're doing great."

Ainslee fell back against the pillows and let go of both Anabelle's and Doug's hands, but another contraction gripped her before she'd had a chance to catch her breath. "Oh no." She snatched their hands up again, and Anabelle used her free one to support Ainslee's leg that was shaking with exhaustion. She shot a look at Doug, who had a look of terror in his eyes.

"You're doing great," Anabelle said to Ainslee.

"It hurts," she moaned.

"Is this normal?" Doug asked.

Dr. Carpenter exchanged a quick knowing glance with Anabelle. "Completely. You're both doing great."

"It's worse than the videos," he said.

She turned her attention back to Ainslee and tried not to grimace as her daughter's nails dug into her hand.

"Very good," Dr. Carpenter said. "You're just a push or two away."

"Really?" Ainslee fell back again but didn't let go of Anabelle's and Doug's hands this time. As another contraction seized her, she squeezed her eyes closed. "Oh, oh, oh," she called out.

"Here comes your baby," Dr. Carpenter said. "Keep pushing."

Anabelle took half a step forward. The baby's forehead was wrinkly and a little bluish. Dr. Carpenter deftly slipped her finger around the baby's neck and looped the cord away. "Ainslee, keep going, your baby is here."

Tears filled Anabelle's eyes as Ainslee pushed forward with all her might. Dr. Carpenter slid her hands onto the baby's shoulders and began to pull. In a whoosh, the baby delivered.

"It's a girl!" Dr. Carpenter announced.

Ainslee fell back against the bed. "Is she okay?"

"She looks great," Dr. Carpenter said, holding the baby as she directed Doug to cut the cord.

Anabelle held her breath and stared in wonderment. Her granddaughter let out a wail as the doctor rubbed her chest.

"Can I see her?" Ainslee asked.

Anabelle's heart felt as if it might burst as Dr. Carpenter laid the baby across her daughter's chest and then covered them both with a cotton blanket. Doug leaned down to his wife and daughter, and Anabelle fumbled for her camera and began taking photos. "She's looking at you—at both of you," she said, snapping away as the wee one, with her dark, dark eyes, squinted against the bright hospital lights and looked first at her mother and then her father.

"Hi, Baby," Ainslee said. "I'm so happy you're here. We're all so happy you're here."

Anabelle kept clicking the shutter on the camera, but all she could see were the tears filling her eyes.

Twenty minutes later, once Dr. Carpenter and Candace had Ainslee cleaned up, Anabelle asked Candace to tell Cameron, Kirstie, Evan, and Louise and George to come in and meet the baby. As she waited, she took the opportunity to speak quietly to her daughter.

"I didn't mean to be critical," Anabelle said. "You're going to be an amazing mother. I've never doubted that for a second."

Ainslee reached for her mother's hand, but before they could say any more the door flew open and Cameron appeared, followed by Kirstie and then Evan and then the Giffens. Anabelle stepped away from the bed and tried not to cry as she photographed the others crowding around the bed. Cameron put down the sparkling cider and cups and whispered, "Hello, Wee One." Then he said he detected a hint of red in the baby's dark hair. Evan patted her head as if she were a kitten, and Kirstie said, "Oh, Ainslee, you always did get the best dolls." Louise had her hands clasped against her breasts, and Anabelle was sure she detected a tear in George's eye.

And all the while, Ainslee looked absolutely beautiful—incredibly exhausted—but glowing, and Doug looked like a man who would take on the world for his baby girl.

"What's her name?" Evan asked, patting Doug on the back.

Anabelle gasped. She hadn't thought to ask!

"Yes," Kirstie said. "Tell us her top secret name."

"Do you want me to say it?" Doug asked, putting his face next to Ainslee's.

"No. I will." She sat up a little straighter, holding the baby close. "Her name is—ta da—Lindsay Belle!" Anabelle captured the moment with a click of the camera.

Kirstie clasped her hands together. "That's beautiful!"

"And the Belle would be for?" Cameron asked.

"Mother." Ainslee was looking straight at Anabelle as she took another photo.

It wasn't until she moved the camera away that the word *Mother* sank in. "For me?" she whispered.

Ainslee nodded and then she said, "Doug could you get a picture of me and Lindsay Belle with Mother?" She winced as she tried to wiggle up straighter.

Anabelle said, "Stop," and adjusted the bed. Then she stepped as close to Ainslee as she could, bent down a little, and smiled toward the camera.

"One, two, three," Doug said and clicked.

Her daughter took her hand again, squeezed it gently, and then slipped Lindsay Belle into the crook of her grandmother's arm.

About the Author

Leslie Gould is the author of eight novels, including five in Guideposts' Home to Heather Creek series. Leslie lives in Portland, Oregon, with her husband and four children. Visit her Web site at www.lesliegould.com.

Read on for a sneak peek of the next exciting and
heartfelt book in *Stories from Hope Haven*.

Available through Guideposts' direct mail program
by calling Customer Service at (800) 932–2145.

Well Wishes
by
Anne Marie Rodgers

ELENA RODRIGUEZ SAT BACK ON HER HEELS IN THE
soft spring grass and brushed the last of the dead
leaves from her tulips. She was relaxed and happy,
delighted that the weather mirrored her fine mood.

It was a beautiful Friday afternoon in early May. Although the
weather still could be chilly in the town of Deerford in north-
central Illinois at this time of year, the past week had been balmy
and mild. Drifts of late tulips in glorious shades of yellow, pink,
and white lent color to the flower beds around Elena's house. She
had the day off work, and as soon as she finished cleaning out
the landscaped beds along the front walk, she was going to begin
cutting the fabric to sew a costume for her granddaughter Isabel,
who was riding on their church's float in the Independence Day
parade in July.

Elena checked her watch. She'd better get cleaned up, or she'd still be covered in soil when her friend Anabelle arrived with a promised costume pattern.

Elena stood. She hefted the handles of the wheelbarrow and began to trundle across the grass. A woman walking along the sidewalk in front of the house caught her eye, and she smiled. "Hello."

"H-hello. Mrs. Rodriguez, may I speak with you?"

Elena searched her memory but couldn't come up with a name. The woman looked familiar, although she was wearing large dark sunglasses that obscured her eyes. "I'm sorry . . . have we met?"

"Yes." It was a whisper, and the woman cleared her throat.

A frisson of awareness danced up Elena's spine as the newcomer turned up the front walkway and approached. Instinctively, Elena tensed. Putting up a hand to block the sun that made a clear view difficult, Elena could see that the stranger was young. She had flyaway blonde hair cut in a short, carefree style that managed to look both messy and attractive at the same time. Small, with narrow shoulders and a fragile air, she had a pretty, heart-shaped face. As the woman removed her sunglasses, Elena could see that the face was dominated by striking silvery gray eyes.

Shock as solid as a body blow hit her at the sight of those eyes. She knew them. She saw them every morning the moment Isabel woke.

"Yes," the young woman said again. "I'm—"

"Sarah," Elena said flatly. "I didn't recognize you."

Sarah Fulton was the last person Elena had expected to see on her suburban street on a sunny spring afternoon. The young woman had been involved with Rafael, Elena's son, six years ago and had given birth to Isabel before she'd run away.

Six years ago, the young woman had sported a long blonde braid and a huge pregnant belly for much of the short time Elena had known her. She had also been so quiet that she'd barely said a word to Elena and Cesar when they rushed to the hospital after getting word that Rafael was about to be a father. In the days after Izzy's birth, Sarah had only grown more withdrawn; and Elena had learned that the young woman had a drug habit that she wouldn't—or couldn't—give up. And then Sarah had disappeared.

Since then, Elena had only seen Sarah once. After last autumn's big storm, Sarah had been brought to an emergency triage center set up at the YMCA. Her hair had appeared much darker, soaked and matted to her head. Sarah's eyes had been dulled by pain and clouded by confusion from a head injury, and they'd been closed throughout a great deal of the very short encounter. Elena had been stunned—she had thought Sarah was long gone from Deerford. When the girl had vanished again, Elena had been relieved beyond measure and had put Sarah out of her mind.

Now she looked at the young woman with apprehension knotting her stomach.

Uncertainty pierced the roiling mass of emotion. "What do you want?" The question sounded abrupt and rude, even to Elena.

"I'd like to speak with you." Sarah sounded as nervous and anxious as Elena felt.

Elena took a deep breath, holding back all the unkind sentiments that wanted to fly out of her mouth as adrenalin rushed through her. "What do you want to talk about?" Elena saw Anabelle's late model silver Ford glide to the curb. *Oh, great.* "I'm sorry. This isn't a good time."

"Please. It will only take a few minutes."

"I don't have a few minutes." Her voice shook with anger and indignation. "You don't belong here. You made your choice when you walked away."

"You don't understand." Sarah's forehead was furrowed with distress.

"I *do* understand," Elena broke in, a fierce motherly love infusing every word. "I picked up the pieces after you broke my son's heart and left my granddaughter motherless. Do *not* tell me I don't understand."

A charged silence fell. Anabelle shut her car door and walked toward them, carrying a plate of what looked like cookies. "Hello!"

Elena cleared her throat and reached for composure. "Hi, Anabelle."

Anabelle patted the quilted carryall on her shoulder. "I have that pattern you asked about, and I found two others that you might like." She stopped beside Sarah, her eyes inquisitive.

"This is Sarah Fulton," Elena said. "Sarah, Anabelle Scott." It was barely gracious, and she saw Anabelle's eyebrows shoot up as her friend recognized the name. Anabelle's expression grew intent, and she turned to give the young woman a closer examination.

Reaching out, Elena took Sarah's elbow and turned her around, practically marching the younger woman down the path to the sidewalk.

"Please leave," she said, the tight fist of anxiety squeezing her heart. She had never been so ungracious in her life, but she had no intention of entertaining this woman's whims. "We don't have anything to talk about."

Sarah turned to face her with a new look of resolve. "*You* may not, but I do." Her voice had grown firm. "I'm back in Deerford to stay." Tears filled her eyes, ruining her assertive posture. "I want to talk with you about becoming a part of Isabel's life," she said in a smaller voice. "Please, Mrs. Rodriguez. I've already missed so much. Can't we just talk?"

Indeed, Sarah had missed so much. She had left a few days following Isabel's birth. Walked away from Rafael and their new baby daughter, abandoned them without even a good-bye other than a single short note. They had never heard from her again until she had called Elena before Isabel's birthday last September. She'd asked to attend the little girl's party. She'd never followed through with a visit, though, and Elena hadn't been very surprised.

You are a Christian, Elena reminded herself sternly. She had to forgive this girl her wrongdoing, even if she couldn't forget it. Unfortunately, forgiveness sounded like a terribly foreign concept at the moment. And even if Sarah's abandonment could be forgiven, what would her sudden appearance do to Izzy? If Sarah really did want to be in Isabel's life, how would that affect Cesar and Elena's close relationship with their precious granddaughter? Since Sarah had abandoned Rafael and

Izzy, Elena had grown used to thinking of her family in terms of "my." *My husband and my son and my granddaughter . . . the four of us . . .*

"I can't do this right now," Elena reiterated. "Give me a number where I can reach you, and I'll think about it."

But as Sarah dug out a pen and a scrap of paper and wrote down a cell phone number, Elena was certain that unless she was forced to, she wouldn't be calling that number anytime soon.

Trying to remain unobtrusive, Anabelle watched thoughtfully as Elena conversed with Sarah Fulton down by the sidewalk. Elena looked stiff, and she leaned forward a little, her body language radiating aggression. Anabelle was surprised to see the normally affectionate woman in such a posture, but she couldn't blame her. If Isabel were Anabelle's granddaughter, she'd be terribly upset too.

After another moment, Elena made an impatient gesture toward the house. Sarah dug in her handbag and brought out paper and pen. Writing something down, she gave the paper to Elena, who accepted it, then turned her back on the woman.

Sarah stood watching Elena walk away, and her face wore one of the saddest expressions Anabelle had ever seen. Pity tugged at her heart, pulling it in two directions.

Elena had raised Izzy from the very first day of her life, when Sarah hadn't wanted to, according to Elena. But Sarah must feel something for her child if she was here again, presumably trying to reconnect. It promised to be a difficult time, with no happy ending in sight for everyone.

When Elena reached Anabelle, she looked so distressed that Anabelle automatically put a supportive arm around her friend. "Come on. Let's go inside."

"You'll get dirty," Elena protested even as she leaned into her friend's embrace.

"I'll wash." Anabelle opened the door and waited while Elena went to her bedroom. She returned in a few moments wearing a fresh white eyelet blouse and a pretty knee-length skirt in a pin-striped pattern with her face and hands washed.

"Did you make those?" Anabelle asked, gesturing to Elena's clothes.

Her friend nodded, her shoulders relaxing incrementally. "Just the skirt. I love this stretch denim fabric. I bought two colors," she added, sounding almost guilty.

"It's made up beautifully," Anabelle said.

"Thank you. Would you like a glass of lemonade or sweet tea?"

"Sweet tea would be great." Anabelle fanned herself with her hand. "I love this warm weather, but I'm not quite used to it after that last cold snap we had."

Anabelle kept the conversation innocuous, sensing that her friend needed a few moments to compose herself. She searched for a new topic. "I spoke to Ainslee this morning. She took Lindsay for a checkup yesterday." Two weeks ago, Anabelle's daughter Ainslee had given birth to Anabelle's first grandchild. They lived only a short distance from Anabelle's little farm, which was located just outside Deerford.

"And?"

"The doctor was pleased. Lindsay gained half a pound."

"Sounds as if she's doing great." Elena's smile was genuine. "You're so lucky. Having a baby around is so wonderful. I adore Izzy, but I do miss those baby days."

"I haven't seen very much of her." Anabelle shook her head. "Ainslee's very protective."

"Protective? With you?"

"Oh, you know . . . concerned about germs, concerned about too much handling, that sort of thing." She made herself smile and shrug. "Typical new mother anxiety." The last thing she wanted to do was unburden her own concerns when Elena was so clearly distressed by Sarah's recent appearance. She turned to the purpose of their get-together, handing Elena the patterns she had brought. "Here you go."

"These are excellent." But Elena's response was distinctly halfhearted. Anabelle's friend traced a pattern on the front of the package with a fingertip. "I guess you know who that visitor was."

"I recognized the name," Anabelle admitted. Since Elena had brought up the subject, she decided it was okay to ask questions. "Why did she come here?"

"She wants to see Izzy, be part of her life. She says she's moving back here for good."

"Oh." Anabelle was stunned. "Moving back here from where?"

"I don't even know. I was so shocked I just wanted her to go away. I told her I couldn't talk to her."

"I would have been shocked too."

They sat in silence for a moment.

"I did get her cell phone number," Elena volunteered. "I'm going to have to deal with her sooner or later."

Anabelle wanted to urge her friend to take action—to call Sarah and schedule a meeting, to find out exactly what the young woman had in mind. If it were her, Anabelle would want to know exactly what she was facing. But she sensed Elena didn't want to acknowledge that Sarah might try to become a permanent part of the Rodriguez family's life.

Although, the girl had pulled a disappearing act more than once. Perhaps she would do it again. Anabelle was certain that Elena was hoping for exactly that event to occur.

"I wish she would just go away again," Elena said, confirming Anabelle's instincts. Her words tumbled over each other, as if she couldn't utter them fast enough. "I'm not going to tell Rafael she was here. She'll probably take off again, and I'll just get him all upset for nothing, right? I'll have to tell Cesar, because he'll take one look at my face and know something is wrong, but Cesar won't say anything to Rafael either. Do you think I'm wrong for keeping it from him?"

"It sounds as if you want to wait and see if she's going to be staying in Deerford." Anabelle thought it was a bad idea to keep the information from Rafael, but Elena was so upset that there was no way Anabelle could tell her that right now.

"Exactly!" Elena acted as if Anabelle had just endorsed her decision. "And really, I'm sure she won't be here long. There's no need to get everyone worked up for no reason." Anabelle hoped Elena was right. But the young woman to whom she'd been introduced did not look like a vagabond or a drug addict. She had been well groomed and neatly dressed. Her skin was clear and pretty, her figure trim and well toned. And she hadn't backed away from Elena's aggressive posture but had held her ground without flinching. There had been a calm resolve in the striking light gray eyes that had reminded Anabelle of Izzy at her most determined. And Isabel Rodriguez, at her most determined, was already a formidable force at the ripe old age of five-and-a-half.

No, Anabelle wasn't sure at all that Sarah Fulton would be leaving Deerford anytime soon.

A Note from the Editors

Guideposts, a nonprofit organization, touches millions of lives every day through products and services that inspire, encourage and uplift. Our magazines, books, prayer network and outreach programs help people connect their faith-filled values to their daily lives.

Your purchase of *Stories from Hope Haven* does make a difference! To comfort hospitalized children, Guideposts Outreach has created Comfort Kits for free distribution. A hospital can be a very scary place for sick children. With all the hustle and bustle going on around them, the strange surroundings, and the pain they're experiencing, is it any wonder kids need a little relief?

Inside each easy-to-carry Comfort Kit is a prayer card, a journal, a pack of crayons, an "I'm Special" wristband to wear alongside the hospital-issued one and a plush golden star pillow to cuddle. It's a welcome gift and has a powerful effect in helping to soothe a child's fears.

To learn more about our many nonprofit outreach programs, please visit www.guidepostsfoundation.org.